NANCY DREW

girl detective™

Once Upon a Crime

CAROLYN KEENE

Super Mystery #2

Truth Is Stranger Than Fiction

by Hazel Perrault
special to the Bugle

Once upon a time, when my life first became entwined with that of young Nancy Drew, I knew little of real-life crime. My life to that point had been rather quiet and cerebral with a decided absence of dark criminal presence anywhere but within my imagination and research—and the pages of my books, of course. I spent much of my time scribbling my humble stories, and the rest occupied in quiet pursuits, such as gardening, cooking, and needlework. I have been fortunate in that my books have been well-received, which has allowed me the luxury of such hobbies—with plenty left over for my beloved charitable causes. I suppose one could say that's when Ms. Drew came in....

NANCY DREW
girl detective™
Super Mystery

#1 Where's Nancy?

#2 Once Upon a Crime

Available from Aladdin Paperbacks

NANCY DREW girl

Super Mystery

Once Upon a Crime

Carolyn Keene

Aladdin Paperbacks
New York   London   Toronto   Sydney

This book is a work of fiction. Any references to historical events, real people, or real locales are used fictitiously. Other names, characters, places, and incidents are the product of the author's imagination, and any resemblance to actual events or locales or persons, living or dead, is entirely coincidental.

☛ ALADDIN PAPERBACKS
An imprint of Simon & Schuster Children's Publishing Division
1230 Avenue of the Americas, New York, NY 10020
Copyright © 2006 by Simon and Schuster, Inc.
All rights reserved, including the right of reproduction in whole or in part in any form.
NANCY DREW is a registered trademark of Simon & Schuster, Inc.
ALADDIN PAPERBACKS, NANCY DREW: GIRL DETECTIVE, and colophon are trademarks of Simon & Schuster, Inc.
Manufactured in the United States of America
First Aladdin Paperbacks edition June 2006
10 9 8 7 6 5 4 3 2
Library of Congress Control Number 2005930882
ISBN-13: 978-1-4169-1248-4
ISBN-10: 1-4169-1248-7

Contents

Once Upon a Time in River Heights

And *as she crept along* the dank, candlelit passage, her terrified heart threatened to leap straight out of her body and through the silky fabric of her hand-stitched Parisian gown. The killer could be anywhere within the manor, skulking among the bins of potatoes and bags of flour in the kitchen; peering out through the cloudy, age-worn panes of the north tower; or perhaps lurking right there in the dim, shadowy passageway beneath the moat. For all she knew he might well be watching her at this very moment with merciless, waiting eyes. The shadows shifted and she gasped, expecting any moment to feel a warm breath on the back of her neck beneath the loose tendrils of her upswept auburn hair. She leaped like a nervous doe as, with a faint sputtering sound, the nearest candle went dark. Even as she assured herself that it was merely the work of a mischievous and unlucky *breeze, not an uncommon event in these ancient, drafty corridors, the sudden sound of footsteps echoed off the stones just behind her. . . .*

"What are you reading, Nancy?"

I glanced up at my friend Bess Marvin, startled out of the romantic world of helpless heroines and mysterious châteaus by her question. "This," I said, holding up the book so Bess could see the cover. "It's Hazel Perrault's latest release."

"Hazel Perrault?" George Fayne wrinkled her nose as she wandered toward us from the computers-and-technology section of the university bookstore. "Isn't that the woman who writes those superflowery historical mysteries? I mean, everyone knows Nancy Drew loves a mystery. But *that* kind of mystery?"

Bess giggled as George rolled her eyes. They both knew there was nothing I liked more than a good mystery. I'd been solving local crimes and puzzles for as long as I could remember. But being my life-long best friends, they also knew I wasn't exactly the fantasy-and-fairy-tales type. I'm a practical girl all the way—if it doesn't make sense, I don't do it, and if it isn't comfortable, I won't wear it.

"Next thing you know she'll be dressing in ballgowns and swooning around town, searching for her fairy godmother or something," Bess joked.

"Thou art indubitably correct, dearest cousin," George replied in a high-pitched voice, dropping into a dramatic curtsy.

"Okay, okay," I said patiently as they continued to snort with laughter. "I know Perrault's writing style can be a little over the top. But her mystery plots are rock solid. And isn't that the most important part in a mystery novel? I believe that's really why her books are all bestsellers—not all the romantic fairy-tale trappings. Anyway, you know what they say about not judging a book by its cover."

"Good thing you feel that way." With a smirk George nodded toward the cover of the book I was holding. It featured a beautiful, moist-eyed young woman dressed in an elaborate pink satin gown, running across the drawbridge of a gloomy-looking manor house. Or maybe it was supposed to be silk—I wouldn't know. I leave such fashion distinctions up to Bess, who is much more interested in that sort of thing than I am.

Bess and George were clearly ready to keep rolling with the jokes, but at that moment the sound of raised voices interrupted our conversation. I glanced over and saw a dark-haired girl my own age, standing in front of the sales counter with a sour look on her pretty face.

"What in the world is Deirdre doing here?" George commented with distaste.

I could understand her surprise. Deirdre Shannon wasn't the type of girl to spend much time browsing in bookstores. Expensive clothing stores, yes. The makeup counter at high-end department stores, sure. Olde River Jewelers on River Street, definitely. But the university bookstore? Not so much. The only book she might be interested in reading would probably be one called *Everything I Need to Know I Learned at the Country Club.*

She certainly didn't seem happy to be there at the moment. Her green eyes flashed as she harangued the clerk, a plump young woman wearing a university T-shirt.

"And if you can't even get the magazine in on time, you might as well not stock it at all," Deirdre was saying irritably, her shrill voice carrying easily throughout the quiet store. "What good does the latest fashion news do me when it's like a week late?"

"I'm sorry," the hapless clerk said, hurrying toward a large magazine rack a few yards from where we were standing. "But are you positive it wasn't there? I'm sure we must have gotten it in. . . ."

Deirdre let out a snort. "I'm sure you haven't," she snipped gracelessly. "But that's only typical of this dull town. It's going to be totally embarrassing to even *attempt* to entertain my cousin Ashley when she comes to visit in a few weeks. She's from Chicago—of the Chicago Shannons, you know—so she's not used

4

to dealing with the limitations of this kind of back-woods burg."

I rolled my eyes. Only Deirdre would consider River Heights, a booming manufacturing town with a population of about twenty-five thousand, a "back-woods burg." It's actually quite a diverse place thanks to all the people who moved here because of Rackham Industries, which is a huge, worldwide supplier of computer parts. The city has a university, several hospitals, a convention center, all sorts of restaurants and specialty shops, and even a small airport. Okay, so it's not Chicago. But it's not exactly Boondocksville, either—except maybe in Deirdre's narrow mind.

"Anyway," I told my friends, raising my voice to be heard above Deirdre's grumbling, "Hazel Perrault definitely ranks as one of my favorite mystery authors. But even if I didn't like her books, I'd still think she was cool, thanks to the work she did to bring the Riverside arsonist to justice a few years back. Remember?"

"Oh, right," George said. "That was the guy who kept burning stuff down over in East Bank and Trib Falls and all those other little towns downriver, right?"

I nodded. "Ms. Perrault was doing research for one of her novels—*Mystery on Misty Moor*, I think it was—when she stumbled across some new evidence in the case. She followed up on it, and her work helped law enforcement capture the culprit."

5

"Jordan Q. Jefferson," George said. "That was the guy's name, right?"

"I think so." I glanced at her with respect. Whenever I start to believe that George doesn't think about anything other than her latest practical joke or where she's going to get the money to buy her next computer gadget, she surprises me. She has a great memory for details . . . that is, when she's paying attention.

Meanwhile Bess was paging through Hazel Perrault's novel, which she'd taken from me. She paused on the back flap. "It's so weird," she commented. "Her books always seem to be set in old ruined castles or haunted forests or other fairy-tale kinds of places. And yet she turns out to be the one who solves the real-life crime—the inspiration for the mystery. Sort of sounds like a movie or something."

"I guess so." I shrugged. "But the real-life fact is, without Ms. Perrault the crime might never have been solved—and Jefferson might still be out there burning down buildings."

"Excuse me, but I couldn't help overhearing your conversation."

I glanced over my shoulder. The young sales clerk was standing there smiling tentatively at us. Deirdre was sullenly paging through magazines nearby. If she'd even noticed we were there, she hadn't given any indication of it. That was no surprise. My friends and I aren't Deirdre's biggest fans, and the feeling is mutual.

"I didn't mean to eavesdrop, but I just heard you mention Ms. Perrault, and I thought you might be interested in something," the clerk went on earnestly. "It was just in the university paper—she's joining forces with Rags 2 Riches for a big fund-raising project down in Tributary Falls. It sounds really cool."

"What kind of project?" I asked, already interested. Rags 2 Riches was a large local charity group. I volunteered for them from time to time, and my father had done some pro bono legal work for them in the past. Most of the big companies in town have sponsored at least one of the group's fund-raisers or other projects. Even Deirdre's father, a wealthy attorney *not* known for his charitable spirit, is on R2R's board of directors.

"They're going to refurbish this rundown movie theater," the clerk said. "I think they want to turn it into a community center for girls. Or something like that. Anyway, they're looking for volunteers to help with the rebuilding and redecorating. Then at the end of the project there's going to be a big fund-raising gala. Hazel Perrault is going to host it, along with her son."

Bess gasped. "You mean Jake Perrault, the actor? He's gorgeous!"

"That guy who starred in *Rebel From the Ashes*?" George snorted. "Yeah, right. Since when do you like the bad-boy type, Bess?"

7

"I don't care about type." Bess sighed dreamily. "But I *do* care about gorgeous green eyes . . . and silky black hair . . . and beautiful, long eyelashes . . ."

The sales clerk shivered appreciatively. "I know," she said. "He's a total hottie."

"The *hottest*." Bess giggled. "Can you imagine dancing with him at some big, romantic ball? Total swoon moment!"

"She said fund-raiser, not ball," George corrected. "I think you've been looking at that Hazel Perrault book cover a little too long, Bess."

I wasn't really listening to their bickering. Unlike Bess, I wasn't that interested in fund-raising balls or handsome movie stars. But I *was* interested in the Rags 2 Riches project. It sounded like a worthwhile way to help people, which was right up my alley. Plus it would mean a chance to meet one of my literary idols at the same time.

I mentioned as much to my friends. "I think I'm going to look into volunteering for this. What could be better? It's a dream opportunity."

George laughed. "Okay, so your idea of a dream opportunity is hammering and sawing all day for no money?" she said. "Hmm. Call me crazy, but it doesn't exactly sound like a fairy tale come true to me."

"What about you?" I turned expectantly to Bess,

8

figuring she would be an easier sell on the idea. Not only was she already fantasizing about meeting Jake Perrault, but she's also surprisingly handy with tools and carpentry.

"Sure," Bess said immediately. "Sounds great."

George frowned. "Well, if you're both going, I guess I will too," she grumbled. "How long will we be stuck on construction duty?"

"I don't know." I smiled at the sales clerk. "You don't happen to still have that newspaper article handy, do you?"

"Sure," she replied. "I wish I could go, too. But I could never get enough time off work."

We headed over to the sales register. The clerk pulled out that day's campus newspaper from underneath the counter. Sure enough, there was a big headline about the R2R project on the front page.

"Oh, no!" Bess cried as soon as she saw the dates. "George and I can't go!"

"What?" I was surprised and disappointed. "Why not?"

"That's the week my parents and George's parents are going to that Marvin family reunion-vacation in Bermuda," Bess explained as George nodded.

I vaguely remembered hearing my friends' parents talking about the trip. Bess's father and George's mother were brother and sister, and this was some kind of long-planned get-together for family members of their generation.

"So?" I prompted, not sure why that should interfere with our plans.

"It's also the week I'm scheduled to get my wisdom teeth out," George said, grimacing. "Bess already promised to stay with me, since you all know I don't deal well with that sort of thing."

Bess grinned. "True," she said. "But George is only one of the babies I'm sitting for that week. I also promised to watch Maggie and Scott." Bess's sister, Maggie, and George's brother Scott were both middle-schoolers and thus a bit too young to stay home alone for that long.

"Oh well," I said with a sigh, the images of working alongside my friends dissipating as fast as they'd come. "Maybe Ned will go with me . . ."

"I still can't believe you're going to be gone for almost a whole week," Ned Nickerson grumbled.

I glanced up from examining the local hardware store's selection of work gloves to smile sympathetically at my boyfriend. "Five days," I told him. "That's all. I wish you could come along. But you'll be so busy with work that you probably won't even miss me."

No matter what kind of brave face I tried to put on, though, I knew I would miss him. After my friends had bailed, I'd inserted Ned in their place in my daydreams—the thought of dancing with him had made me look forward to the fund-raising ball almost as much as the project itself.

Unfortunately none of those dreams were going to come true, either. During breaks from his studies at the university, Ned worked for his father, the publisher of the *River Heights Bugle*. Normally his schedule there was fairly flexible, but he had promised to cover a series of political meetings that happened to be taking place the same week as the R2R project.

He reached over and squeezed my shoulder. "I'll miss you like crazy. Anyway, this project must be cursed or something. What are the odds that Bess and George can't go that week, either?"

I laughed. "Well, I don't believe in curses," I said. "But it certainly is bad luck. I wish you guys could come along, but it's still a great cause, and it will be awesome having the chance to meet Hazel Perrault. I can't wait to ask her about her work, and . . ."

My voice trailed off as I blinked in surprise at the unusual vision before me. Deirdre had just entered the store, trailed by a tall, slender girl with sleek blond hair and a haughty expression. If there was one place Deirdre Shannon belonged in even less than a bookstore, it was a hardware store. In her stylish leather bolero jacket and expensive sandals, she stood out among the saw blades and hammers like a proverbial sore thumb.

Ned blinked at the pair in obvious surprise. "Do my eyes deceive me or is that Deirdre? Do you think she's lost?" he wondered.

"Excuse me!" Deirdre called loudly in the general direction of the store's front counter. "We need some help over here. It's very important."

"That must be the famous cousin Ashley," I murmured to Ned, nodding toward the other girl.

"Yeah," Ned agreed. "And she doesn't exactly look like the handy type, either."

That was true enough. Both Deirdre and her cousin were dressed to the nines, complete with stylish handbags and full makeup.

"Maybe they got lost on the way to some hip new restaurant, and they're just in here asking for directions," I whispered, only half kidding. I really couldn't imagine why else they would be in the hardware store.

"The work gloves are right over here," a sales clerk said as he led the girls toward the aisle where Ned and I were standing.

Deirdre's eyes lit up as she approached us, though it had nothing to do with the store's wide selection of sturdy work gloves. She had just spotted Ned.

I hid a smile by leaning down to pick up another pair of gloves. Deirdre has had the hots for Ned for as long as any of us can remember. She seems to take his politeness for encouragement. She never gives up on trying to charm Ned—not even when I'm standing right there with him.

"Hello, Ned," Deirdre cooed. "I don't think you've met my cousin Ashley. She's visiting from Chicago for a couple of weeks. Ash, this is Ned Nickerson. He's the most promising young newsman in River Heights—he could probably get a job in, like, Chicago or New York, even." As I straightened up again, she shot me a dismissive glance. "Oh, and that's Nancy. She went to school with me."

"Charmed, whatever." Cousin Ashley sounded bored. "Come on, Deirdre. Let's get the stuff we need and get out of here. I need to get a pedicure before we leave town."

"Okay." Deirdre was still smiling beguilingly at Ned. "So, Ned, what brings you in here? Are you planning some kind of home-improvement project or something?"

"Nope, nothing like that," Ned replied mildly. "I'm just helping Nancy shop for a few building supplies. She's volunteering for a project down in Trib Falls— R2R's going to be fixing up an old movie theater this week."

Deirdre traded a smug smile with her cousin before turning back to Ned and me.

"We know," she said. "We're going too."

...and one of the last spots to fall victim to the Riverside Arsonist's flame was the venerable Chateau Theater of Tributary Falls. Located on a spit of land just across the creek from the main part of town, the theater dripped with old-world style from its lush red velvet seats to the real butter on the popcorn. Alas the arsonist's spark put an end to that legacy.

However, the brave and noble volunteers of the local fire company managed to save the shell of the building, and experts had since declared it safe and a good candidate for refurbishment. When I heard about it, I simply couldn't resist

the romance of the majestic old place—or the opportunity to give it a second chance at a useful life.

It was most gratifying to find that so many people were willing, even eager, to put their lives on hold for a week to lend their strength, expertise, and enthusiasm to the project. The Rags 2 Riches group, based in River Heights, advertised for volunteers, and before I knew it, these generous souls were gathered together, ready to meet the challenge. Their only reward would be hard work and the satisfaction of a job well done, and their only motive was generosity. Or so I believed at first . . .

2

What's in a Name?

I leaned back against the seat of Ned's car, staring out at the passing scenery. We had just entered Tributary Falls, a sleepy little town about a third of the size of River Heights, whose claims to fame were its old brick clock tower and an odd preponderance of shoe stores. Ned and I had spent most of the hourlong drive chatting about the project, George's oral surgery, and other topics.

With a shiver, I realized we were almost there. "This is going to be so cool," I murmured, watching the stores and restaurants of the shopping district slide by outside the car window. Then I sighed, the sight of an expensive boutique bringing me back to reality. "It's just too bad Deirdre's the only person I know who's going."

15

"And Cousin Ashley," Ned reminded me with a slight smile. "Don't forget about her."

I groaned. "I was trying to," I muttered. "I still can't believe those two are actually doing this. My guess is that Mr. Shannon has something to do with it. It's not like Deirdre to volunteer for physical labor like this."

"You're probably right. Then again, maybe Cousin Ashley is a paragon of charitable spirit and this was all her idea," Ned argued with a smile.

Even though I knew he was joking, I answered seriously. "That's true," I said. "We really shouldn't judge by appearances—just because Cousin Ashley *looks* like a shallow, self-centered Deirdre-clone doesn't necessarily mean it's true." I shrugged. "But I still think the most likely solution to this little mystery is that Mr. S. thinks it'll look good for his business if his daughter and niece volunteer. He probably 'convinced' them to go along with it by promising to buy them each a new car or something."

"I'm sure the chance to meet a movie star had something to do with their willingness, too," Ned said as he eased to a stop at a traffic light on Prince Street.

"Good point," I agreed. "Especially a hunky one like Jake Perrault. The three of them will probably get along great—they can all discuss the newest hair conditioner and the latest Hollywood gossip."

Ned didn't answer. The light had turned green

16

again, and he was slowly driving down the next block. There wasn't much traffic at that hour on a Monday morning, and he was able to take his time to look for the address we needed.

"I think this is it," he said, peering up to the left.

I leaned across him to look. Ned had just stopped in front of a large, gray, stone building with a neon sign reading **PALACE HOTEL** in old-fashioned, fancy, script letters. Staring up at the façade, I felt a shiver of excitement pass through me. This was going to be a once-in-a-lifetime experience, and I wasn't about to let Deirdre Shannon ruin my fun.

After saying good-bye to Ned, I entered the hotel's hushed, carpeted lobby. A doorman took my bags and pointed me toward the open doors of the main conference room, where a handful of people were clustered near the small stage set up on one side of the large, open space. I entered and spotted Deirdre and her cousin—or, rather, I *heard* them—almost immediately. The shrill sound of giddy laughter echoed through the nearly empty room, immediately turning the cousins into the center of attention. The two of them were standing with a very tall, very slender woman dressed in an elegant linen pantsuit. She was in her midthirties and looked vaguely familiar, though I couldn't place her face right away. I wondered if I'd encountered her on previous R2R projects.

17

Glancing around I took in the rest of the faces in the ballroom. A fiftyish-looking man dressed in overalls and work boots was standing alone near the wall, while a much younger but similarly dressed man picked over the offerings on a refreshments table. A trio of girls, probably about fourteen years old, were giggling among themselves near the restrooms. My heart sank slightly as I realized Deirdre and her cousin were the only people my age in the room. Somehow I'd been imagining a big project with dozens of volunteers of all ages. Were more people still on the way or was this it?

Oh well. Either way, if I was going to be stuck with them, I figured I might as well try to play nice. Taking a deep breath, I headed toward them to say hello.

Just then I heard footsteps hurrying into the room. Turning I saw a petite sixtysomething woman entering. I gasped. Hazel Perrault looked just like she did on her book jackets, from her unruly gray curls to her flowing purple shawl and sensible shoes.

Forgetting all about Deirdre and company, I hurried over to introduce myself. "Ms. Perrault," I said, feeling a little breathless all of a sudden. It's not often that I get to meet one of my heroes. "It's so great to meet you. My name is Nancy Drew—I'm one of the volunteers for this project."

The older woman's smile put me at ease immediately. "Of course," she said, reaching out and grasping one of my hands in both of hers. Her skin felt soft and wrinkly, like the worn old pages of a favorite book. "Miss Nancy Drew. I have read of your wonderful mystery-solving skills in the papers many times, my dear. I'm honored to have you here."

I blushed, a little surprised that a mystery writer as famous as Hazel Perrault had heard of my modest small-town exploits. "The honor's all mine, Ms. Perrault," I said. "I adore your books. *Blood In the Moat* was one of the best mysteries I've ever read. Oh, and I thought it was so cool how you helped the police capture the Riverside arsonist . . ."

She modestly waved away my praise. "That was pure chance," she said. "But I'm so pleased to hear that you enjoy my writing. I always fear that younger, more modern people are likely to have little interest in my old-fashioned tales of moats and castles and such."

"You write good stories; that's what counts for me. Like I tell my friends, your mystery plots are great." I smiled, thinking back to how engrossed I'd become in her latest paperback a couple of months earlier. "Besides, even a modern girl can identify with the people in your books. Everybody knows how scary it is to be somewhere all alone and cut off from everything familiar, whether they're in some isolated castle in the middle of the moors or in a parking garage in the bad part of town."

She chuckled. "Thank you for your kind words, my dear. But I do hope you won't find this project too frightening. The old theater we'll be working in is a bit isolated—just like the tower in my latest book." Her intelligent gray eyes twinkled behind her wire-rimmed glasses. "I trust that won't scare you off."

"It takes more than that to scare me," I replied playfully. "But I thought the burned-out theater was right here in town. I didn't realize it was out in the middle of nowhere."

"It's not, really." She sighed. "The Chateau Theater was once the finest movie house in the county—people came from as far away as Silver Creek or River Heights to enjoy a special show there. It's located on a narrow island between two smallish branches of the big river—these twin tributaries meet up at the rapids at the bottom of the island, which is how the town got its name."

"Interesting. I've only been to Trib Falls a few times. I don't think I've ever seen that part of town—or been to the Chateau Theater."

She nodded. "That doesn't surprise me. Sadly, even before the fire, the Chateau was only a shadow of its former glory. It had turned into a cheap place to go to see third-rate films. The only other businesses still operating on the island just prior to the fire were a couple of secondhand stores and a betting parlor. Shortly before the

20

arsonist struck, the Carltons—they're the owners of the bed-and-breakfast, where we'll be staying—were hoping to buy up the Chateau and a couple of the other properties and maybe take a shot at gentrifying the whole area. They gave up on that plan after the fire, of course."

"That's too bad. Did the B and B escape the fire, then?"

"Just barely." She shook her head. "It was the only thing on the island that wasn't at least partially burned, mostly thanks to the pond behind it. Even the bridge connecting the island to this side of the river was destroyed. Nobody ever bothered to repair it until now. Like the Chateau, all the other businesses just gave up and left, so it's now a twenty-minute drive back to civilization over the bridge on the far side of the island, which has, until recently, made it difficult to drum up much support for this project. But the new bridge should finally be finished by the end of the week—just in time for the grand opening of our new girls' community center." She smiled brightly, clearly happy to think about all the good we'd be doing that week.

"Well, it sounds like a great project," I said. "And what's more, I bet the fund-raiser at the end will raise tons of money for R2R's other projects."

She hesitated briefly before answering. "Yes," she said slowly. "That will be nice."

21

I blinked, wondering if I was imagining things. Even though I'd just met her, I would have sworn at that moment that Ms. Perrault's smile suddenly looked a bit forced.

Before I could figure out what that was all about, she spoke again, her voice brisker and brighter now. "So, Miss Drew," she said. "I'm fascinated by your amateur detective work. I do hope you'll tell me all about some of the mysteries you've solved. Do you find them, or do they usually find you?"

"Some of each," I replied, half of my mind still focused on her odd expression a moment earlier. "And please, call me Nancy."

"All right, Nancy. And I'm Hazel." She glanced around the room. Nobody else had noticed her arrival yet. Deirdre and Ashley were still chatting with their new friend, and both men and all three teen girls were now gathered around the refreshments table. "I suppose I should bring this little meeting to order so we can get started. Excuse me, Nancy."

"Of course."

Moments later she was calling for attention from the small stage. As the others gathered around, I found myself standing next to the older guy. Other than offering a quick nod, he ignored my presence, along with that of everyone else in the room. There was something about him—he was one of those people who seem to have a sort of force field around them, warning other people to stay away. Still, his eyes looked kind, and his hands showed the evidence of many years of hard physical labor. I had a hunch there might be a kind soul beneath the gruff exterior.

I didn't have time to check out anyone else before I got caught up in what Hazel was saying. She welcomed us to the project, reviewing the information she'd just shared with me. Then she explained the details of the project in more detail. We would be responsible for finishing some light construction work as well as cleaning and decorating the interior spaces and fixing up the surrounding yard and parking lot.

"I'm afraid we'll be working you quite hard this week," she went on. "And I'll be ducking out of most of it." She grinned as we all chuckled. "But in case you need further inspiration, I want to introduce you to three very special girls who will be working right alongside you: Meghan, Lacy, and Audrey, please say hello to everyone."

The trio of teens looked bashful as everyone else turned to look at them. "Hey," said the boldest of the three, a petite girl with tight braids, giving us a jaunty little wave while the other two giggled.

"These girls live right here in Tributary Falls," Hazel continued. "They'll be among those using the new center when it's finished."

"Wait," Cousin Ashley spoke up, sounding slightly bored. "I thought we were building some kind of home for troubled youths or something."

Hazel pursed her lips. "We prefer to call it a community center," she said. "It's a place for girls, like our three friends here, to gather and have fun without the temptations of the street or risking trouble with the law."

Deirdre raised her hand. At Hazel's nod she stepped forward. "Let me get this straight," she said. "You're expecting us to finish building this place and decorate it and everything. And it's just me and Ash, four other regular people, and a bunch of juvenile delinquents?"

The three teens shot her nasty looks, and I hid a smile. That was typical Deirdre—making new friends everywhere she went! I supposed I should be honored that she actually thought of me as a "regular person." Normally I suspected she thought of me in much less polite terms.

Hazel answered the question seriously. "I realize you're a streamlined group," she said. "But I'm confident you can do it. You each have wonderful skills that should help make things go smoothly. For instance, I understand that Ms. Aulnoy has some experience with interior design."

I nodded to myself at the name. *That* was why the tall, thin woman looked so familiar. She was Synndi Aulnoy, a former Miss Midwest and a successful local fashion model. She'd contacted my father recently, wanting him to represent her in her divorce from a wealthy local real-estate magnate. Dad was too busy to take the case, much to fashionista Bess's disappointment, so I'd never actually met Ms. Aulnoy, but I'd seen her photos in catalogs and in the newspaper. I gazed at her curiously, taking in her long, almost bone-thin limbs, her perfectly coiffed black hair, and a red dress that Bess probably would have recognized as some kind of designer original, but that, to me, just looked tight and sort of itchy.

Meanwhile Hazel was introducing the two overall-clad men. The younger one was named Wayne and had been working at various construction jobs for several years.

"And here we have our other construction expert," Hazel continued, turning to smile at the older man. "He was generous enough to take time off from him own construction company to come and help us out. I'm sure we'll all be grateful to have his expertise and work ethic. I'm pleased to introduce Mr. Jordan T. Jefferson. He prefers to be called JT."

For a second I wondered why that name sounded so familiar. Then my eyes widened as the answer came to me. The construction worker had almost the same name as the Riverside arsonist!

3

To the Chateau

The name was an odd coincidence, but I didn't think about it for long. After all, Jefferson wasn't exactly an unusual name. Besides, there were much more interesting things to think about as Hazel finished her introductions and then herded us out to a waiting van. The hotel porters had already loaded our bags into the back, so we all piled in for the ride to the site.

"As I mentioned to some of you already, we have a little bit of a drive to get to the theater," Hazel warned as she settled herself into the front passenger seat. With a smile she reached forward and rapped her knuckles on the faux wooden finish of the dashboard. "At least that's what they tell me."

Deirdre looked up from fastening her seatbelt. She

and Cousin Ashley had snagged the first seat along with their new friend, Synndi Aulnoy, leaving me to squeeze onto the middle seat with Wayne and JT while the three teens climbed into the back. "Wait," Deirdre said. "I thought we were going to our hotel first?"

Ashley glanced out the side window as the van's driver pulled away from the curb. "I don't see why we can't stay here at the Palace," she complained. "It seems decent enough—you know, for a small-town place."

"Oh, I think you'll like the B and B," Hazel said, not seeming to notice their whiny tone. "It's a lovely place. It's been in the Carlton family for generations—that's why they've kept it up all these years, even though they haven't gotten much business since the fire."

"Carlton?" Synndi spoke up, sounding interested. "Would that be Alexander Page Carlton? I know him—he's a friend of my ex. Very rich guy."

"Yes, the Carltons are quite well-to-do." If Hazel was taken aback by Synndi's rather crass comment, she didn't let it show. "That's what has allowed them to maintain the B and B despite the lack of business. They spend most of their time at their home in Chicago, but they keep this place for family holidays and the occasional customer. I think they've hoped the island might someday recover its former glory." She smiled. "Perhaps our little project will help with that."

"Yeah, some recovery," Deirdre muttered, staring

out the window as the van made its way through the sleepy little town. "Bring in a bunch of juvenile delinquents. Sounds fabulous."

"In any case," Hazel went on, ignoring Deirdre's sarcastic comment along with the resulting snorts from the teens in the back, "the Carlton family has been kind enough to turn over the place to us for the duration of this project."

"Whatever." Ashley sounded bored. "As long as there's cable TV and maid service, I can make do."

Hazel cleared her throat. Was it my imagination, or was there a glint of amusement in her eyes? "I'm sorry, my dear," she said. "On both counts. There has been no cable service on the island since the fire. And I'm afraid you'll be in charge of your own cooking and cleaning this week."

I didn't mind that idea at all—it sounded kind of fun to play house in a B and B for a week. But I couldn't help being amused at the matching expressions of shock and horror on the faces of Deirdre and her cousin as they turned to stare at each other. You would have thought they'd just been told they were expected to kill their own dinner with their bare hands every night.

Hazel quickly changed the subject, talking about all the good work Rags 2 Riches had done throughout the years. The conversation continued for the next ten minutes or so, when we found ourselves bouncing over a wooden bridge spanning a narrow but fast-moving river.

"Is this thing safe?" Synndi asked, sounding nervous as she peered out the window.

"Been the only crossing to the island since the fire," JT spoke up gruffly. "S'pose it'll hold out a few more days."

He seemed to be right, as the van made it safely to the other side. I stared out the window, curious to see where we would be spending the week.

The island was small—probably not more than a mile from end to end and a bit narrower across—and the whole place looked like the aftermath of a war zone. The road we were on was pitted and cracked, and the charred ruins of a dozen or so buildings, which may have been houses, lined either side. Chunks of debris were scattered everywhere—old drywall, burned-out cars, piles of bricks or stones. Nature had reclaimed much of the mess throughout the past few years. While any large trees that had once grown on the island had burned along with the buildings, nearly every open space was a riot of weeds and wildflowers, and slender saplings poked out of skeletal structures and shaded mounds of old trash.

It wasn't hard to spot the Chateau Theater, since it was the only building on the main road still in one piece. While the basic structure appeared to be sound from what I could tell, the place was a mess. The small, overgrown yard in front was littered with debris, and drifts of ash hid most of the parking lot at one side of the theater. After just one look I could tell it was going to be a challenge to get it all in shape in less than a week.

"Ugh," Deirdre said. "Don't tell me that's what we're supposed to fix up."

"That's it," Hazel replied cheerfully. "Beautiful, isn't it?"

Deirdre shot the older woman a look, clearly uncertain about how to take the comment. That kept Deirdre silent long enough for us to leave the theater behind. Glancing forward, I saw what could only be the Carlton place.

Located about a quarter-mile across an open field from the theater, the bed-and-breakfast was a charming three-story Victorian-style home, complete with gables and shutters and a pretty hedge of roses. Its clean, well-cared-for appearance really stood out in the midst of the burned-out desolation of the rest of the island.

"Cute place," Synndi commented as the van driver pulled into the circular driveway. "Doesn't look very big, though. Are we all going to fit?"

"You should be fine," Hazel assured her. "JT and Wayne live right here in town, so they'll be commuting in each day from their own homes. I've already figured out how to divvy up the rest of you in what I think is a fair and workable way—there are four nicely sized bedrooms."

"Four?" Ashley exclaimed, obviously doing some rapid math in her head. "Hold on. Four bedrooms, and seven people? What is this, summer camp? Prison?"

"Not at all," Hazel replied calmly as the van pulled to a stop. "The girls have already told me they'd like to stay together. They'll be in the largest room, the Sunrise Suite." She nodded toward the young teens, who were already pushing at one another as they clambered for the door. "I understand you and Deirdre are cousins, so I thought the two of you wouldn't mind sharing the Coaching Room. That leaves the remaining two rooms for Synndi and Nancy."

"Oh, okay." Synndi seemed satisfied with that, though Deirdre and Ashley were once again looking dismayed. "Come on, what are we waiting for?"

"Yes, let's go," Hazel agreed, reaching for her door handle. "I should have just enough time to give you a tour of the place before I need to head back into town."

We all climbed out of the van. Deirdre, Ashley, and Synndi headed straight for the front door, but I walked around to the back to get my bag. The driver, a genial-looking older man, shooed me away.

"Go on," he said with a wink. "I'll get the bags. You

31

don't want to miss the tour, or those other girls might decide to switch rooms and stick you in the basement."

I laughed and thanked him, then hurried to catch up to the others. The two construction workers were talking with each other on the front porch, but the rest of the group was clustered in front of the wide double doors. Hazel pulled out a brass key, and a moment later we entered a beautifully decorated front hall dominated by a gorgeous, carved wooden staircase.

"Wow," I said. "It's lucky this place didn't burn—these stairs are amazing!"

"Yeah, great," Deirdre said sourly, showing little interest in the architectural wonders of the house. "Let's go see the bedrooms first, okay? I want to know where I'm supposed to sleep for the next week."

Hazel led the way up the stairs. "Three of the rooms are on this floor," she said. "The Sunrise Suite is on the third floor."

"We get our own floor?" one of the younger girls—I didn't have their names straight yet—spoke up.

"Cool!" one of her friends added with a giggle.

Ashley shot them a slightly sour look. "Yes, well, I hope you're not going to make too much noise up there. I'm a very light sleeper."

Hazel was opening the first door. "This is the Garden Room," she said. "I thought Nancy might like this one." She smiled at me.

I stepped forward to look. "Wow, it's beautiful!" I exclaimed.

The room was small but bright, dominated by a pair of large windows looking out onto the back garden. It was decorated in shades of pink and yellow. The furniture all appeared to be antique—from the comfortable-looking canopy bed to the cozy armchairs in front of the tiled fireplace in one corner. Framed botanical prints lined the walls.

When I turned to smile at Hazel, I saw Deirdre peering into the room with a smirk. "Are you sure you'll be all right in here, Nancy?" she said. "This room is a little girly for you, isn't it?"

I rolled my eyes. "Funny. Come on—after seeing this, I can't wait to check out the rest of the place."

The next room in the hall was identified by a little brass plaque outside as the River Room. It was furnished in soothing shades of blue and green, with decor featuring sailing prints, bottled ships, and similar objects.

"I hope you'll be comfortable in here, Synndi," Hazel said.

"Thank you. I'm sure it will be fine."

Finally we reached the large room at the front of the house known as the Coaching Room. At least twice as large as the others, it was decorated sort of like an old-time men's club with burnished mahogany paneling, hunter-green wallpaper, and lots of leather.

A harness adorned the wall between the double beds, equestrian prints hung here and there, and a collection of antique riding crops and hunting horns filled one section of the bookcase lining one wall.

Ashley wrinkled her nose when she saw the large oil painting hanging above the fireplace mantel, which showed a team of prancing white horses pulling an old-fashioned black carriage.

"Ew," she said. "I can't stay in here. I'm allergic to horses."

Even Deirdre laughed at that one. "I'm sure you'll live, Ash."

Ashley pouted prettily. "Whatever," she muttered. "Is this tour over yet?"

"Just one more room to go," Hazel said. "But you can stay here in your room if you're too tired."

"No, I want to see the rest of the place." Ashley sighed, glancing once more around the Carriage Room as we left.

We headed up another, narrower staircase to the third floor. Hazel pointed out the door to the attic storage space at the back, then led the way to the Sunrise Suite.

As she opened the door, Deirdre blinked in surprise. "Wow," she said. "It looks like a pumpkin exploded in here."

The large space had clearly earned its name thanks

to the huge picture window facing east, which probably offered an amazing view of the sun, rising over the river. The walls and fabrics were all in warm shades of orange and yellow to reflect the theme. The walls really did have a nice pumpkin-y sort of glow, though I doubted Deirdre had meant her comment as a compliment.

"What do you think, girls?" Hazel asked the trio of teens with a smile. "There are only two beds, but we had a cot brought in for you." She pointed to a foldaway bed that had been set up near the window.

"Cool," one of them replied while the others nodded.

As we headed down the stairs, we met the driver bringing the bags up to the second floor, assisted by JT. "I'll get that," I said, reaching for my own suitcase and duffel bag. "Thanks, guys."

"No problem," the driver said cheerfully. "Have a nice stay, ladies."

I lugged my bags into the room and dumped them at the foot of the bed, figuring I could unpack later. At the moment I was more interested in seeing the rest of the house and finding out the schedule for that afternoon's work.

When I emerged into the hall, I noticed that Hazel and the younger girls had disappeared. Deirdre, Ashley, and Synndi were huddled together near the doorway to the Coaching Room, deep in conversation. They all stopped talking and stared at me when I appeared.

"I'm going to go check out the first floor," I said, doing my best to be friendly. I figured it was probably a lost effort with Deirdre and Ashley, but maybe Synndi would turn out to be nice. "Want to come?"

"We'll be there in a minute," Synndi replied with a sweet smile.

Downstairs I found Hazel chatting with the construction workers in the kitchen, which was sunny and spacious. The two men wandered off together, discussing something about drywall tools, and I joined Hazel by the window in the breakfast nook. Glancing out I saw that it offered a view of the theater across an open field.

"Ready for this, Nancy?" Hazel asked.

"I hope so," I replied with a smile. "I'm really looking forward to it."

She sighed. "I only wish I could stay and help," she said. "But I look forward to seeing the results of your hard work at the end of the week—and seeing you all at the fund-raiser, of course."

"That should be fun," I said politely, not wanting to let her know that the big gala fund-raiser sounded a little boring to me now that Ned wasn't going to be there.

Just then we heard the sound of footsteps on the stairs. A moment later Synndi entered the kitchen, followed by Deirdre and Ashley.

"Nice," Synndi said, glancing around the room.

"The pantry and fridge are fully stocked for you," Hazel told her. "If you need anything, I'm sure one of the men can pick it up on his way in from town. Right, guys?"

"Sure thing, Ms. Perrault," Wayne replied from across the room, where he and JT were still talking. "Speaking of, JT and I thought we'd catch the ride with you and head home to clean up before dinner—then we'd head back. I'll drive my truck in; JT doesn't mind walking in when he's ready."

Hazel nodded. "Sounds fine to me."

Just then, the driver strode in. "Ready to go, Ms. P.?" he asked. "We'd better get on the road soon, or you'll miss your flight."

"Ready, Charles." Hazel clasped her hands together and smiled at all of us. "Oh, I do hope you all have fun this week!"

I nodded and smiled. Nearby I noticed Deirdre and her cousin exchanging a dubious glance.

"I want to thank each one of you for volunteering your time, energy, and enthusiasm for this project," Hazel continued. "And I'll see you all at the fundraiser in a few days."

"Your son, Jake, will be there, right?" Deirdre spoke up.

"Yes, of course." Hazel smiled at her. "He's looking forward to it."

Deirdre nodded, looking satisfied. She and Ashley exchanged another glance, making me wonder what they would have done if Hazel had said Jake couldn't make it after all.

Hazel finished her good-byes, and Charles hustled her out of the room, JT and Wayne in tow. She hadn't been gone for more than two minutes when Synndi clapped her hands and called for everyone who was staying in the house to gather in the sitting room, a cozy space at the front of the house that was dominated by a large, brick-lined fireplace. Synndi stood in front of the mantel, impatiently tapping her foot as the rest of us found seats on the overstuffed sofa or the wicker armchairs. The pleasant smile she'd worn throughout the tour was gone, replaced by a steely expression.

"Okay," she said abruptly once she had our attention. "I guess I'm in charge here now that she's gone. And a few things are going to change right away...."

What is it that makes some people believe in Fate, Chance, or Luck, while others see only coincidences or bad choices? It's a question that may never be answered. As for myself, my heart lies somewhere in the middle. In the end most events, whether good or bad, can be traced to a person's action or inaction; a decision made or deferred; a series of choices leading inexorably to a certain result. Then again there are times when life seems unfair, and bad things happen to good people—or good places, as in the case of the Chateau Theater. Is bad luck random? Do some people draw it to themselves like a magnet, through no ill deeds of their own? Or is it all part of some larger purpose or celestial plan?

4

Banished

Half an hour later my head was still spinning from Synndi's changes. The woman had done a Jekyll-and-Hyde-type of transformation upon Hazel's departure, turning from the sweet, polite beauty queen she'd seemed at first into the wicked queen of the castle.

"There are going to be a few changes in the room assignments," she'd announced. "I'm sure Hazel meant well, but her plan just isn't going to work. For one thing, I really think someone needs to stay on site at the theater to keep an eye on things."

I wondered why Synndi was so worried about guarding the theater. Who did she think was going to bother the old, abandoned place? Nobody else lived on the island anymore, and the Riverside Arsonist was in prison.

All such questions flew out of my head at her next words: "I've decided the best person to stay over at the theater is . . . Nancy," she announced.

My jaw dropped as Deirdre and Ashley glanced at me with smug smiles. The teen girls just looked amused.

"I've also decided I'd better stay upstairs in the Sunrise Suite," Synndi continued, not giving me a chance to respond. "I need as much morning light as possible—for health reasons."

"So where are we supposed to sleep?" demanded the boldest of the teens.

"Don't worry, Audrey," Synndi said smoothly. "You three can bunk in the River Room instead."

There was some muttering from the girl who'd spoken—Audrey. I couldn't blame her. The River Room was less than half the size of the Sunrise Suite. It didn't make sense for the three of them to cram in there while Synndi had the whole third-floor suite to herself. But then one of Audrey's friends leaned over and whispered something in her ear. At that, she fell silent immediately.

Synndi had already moved on. "Since Ashley doesn't like horses, she'd better take the Garden Room," she said. "That leaves Deirdre in the Coaching Room . . ."

I'd tried to protest, of course. But it didn't do any

good. I was voted down vigorously by the others. Even the teens suddenly seemed suspiciously supportive of the new plan.

That was how I found myself sitting on a cot in a tiny, windowless room that had once been the ladies' lounge and restroom of the movie theater. A single bare bulb lit up the "lounge" half of the space, which was now my bedroom. It was a far cry from the cozy, comfortable Garden Room. The floor was dingy, heat-curled linoleum; there were spiders in the corners; and a layer of dust and ash covered everything. I could only hope that JT had been right in saying that the plumbing in the bathroom portion of the space had already been repaired.

I was just sitting there on my pathetic, lumpy little cot, staring at my suitcase and wondering how I of all people had been so bulldozed, when Deirdre hurried in without bothering to knock. She had changed clothes since the last I'd seen her, and was now dressed in a polo shirt and a pair of designer jeans.

"Nice place," she said with a quick glance around. "Listen, Synndi sent me over to tell you she just made up the work assignments for the rest of the day."

I suddenly felt a little less glum. What did it matter where I slept? With any luck, I'd be so tired from each day's work fixing up the theater that I'd be asleep before my head hit the pillow. The cause was what mattered, not the accommodations. I glanced at my watch; it was a little before four p.m.—plenty of daylight left for getting started.

"Okay," I said. "What's the plan? Are we starting out in the yard or tackling the interior first?"

"Neither." Deirdre shot me a smug little smile. "At least as far as you're concerned. Your task for tonight is to go back to the B and B and fix dinner for everyone."

"What?" It wasn't exactly what I'd been expecting. I'd signed on to help refurbish the theater, not to play chef.

"Din. Ner." Deirdre pronounced it slowly and carefully. "You know, it's that meal people eat in the evening. You heard the old lady—we're on our own. So Synndi figured, why should everyone waste a lot of time cooking for themselves when we can just have one of us make enough for everyone?"

I had to admit that made sense. And if I got my turn at cooking duty out of the way early, I'd be free to focus on the interesting stuff later.

"All right," I said. "I'm sure I can rustle up something edible. Tell everyone that dinner will be served at, um . . ." I checked my watch again. "Six thirty or so."

"Make it six." Deirdre was already turning to go. "Oh, and Ashley's allergic to onions. And dairy. And don't forget I don't eat red meat."

Just then I heard the front door slam. "I'm back," JT said. "Wayne's not far behind—he's getting out of the truck."

Great. Two more to cook for.

I shook my head, wondering how I was supposed to forget Deirdre's aversion to red meat when I hadn't known it in the first place. But I didn't worry about it for long. It usually doesn't pay to think too hard about anything Deirdre says.

"This is good, Miss Drew," one of the girls—I was pretty sure it was Lacy—said shyly as she reached for a second helping of spaghetti with marinara sauce. "You're a good cook."

I chuckled. "Don't let my friends hear you say that," I joked. "They'll probably die laughing."

Lacy giggled, then turned her attention back to her food. All nine of us were seated at the big oak table in the dining room, which lay between the kitchen and the sitting room. Synndi was at the head of the table with Deirdre and Ashley on either side. JT had taken the chair at the opposite end of Synndi. I was sitting between Deirdre and Wayne, with the three teens across from me.

"So, Deirdre," Synndi was saying. "Are you going to type up the minutes from the decorating meeting?"

"Sure." Deirdre shrugged. "I think I saw a computer

in that little room off from the sitting room. I can type it in there and print out a copy for each of us."

"Good," Synndi said. "Oh, and I saw that computer too. It looks a little out-of-date—hope it still works. Speaking of computers, did I tell you guys about the cool new laptop my boyfriend bought me last month? It was superexpensive, but he says nothing's too expensive for—"

"Decorating meeting?" I interrupted. "When did that happen?"

"When do you think?" Ashley turned and stared at me as if I'd suddenly sprouted an extra head. "We had it while you were cooking. Duh."

I took a deep breath, trying not to let her snotty tone get to me. This whole project would go a lot more smoothly if we could all manage to get along.

"Okay," I said, forcing a smile. "I'd really like to get involved in the decorating too. I have some ideas, and—"

"Excuse me." Synndi's voice was sharp as she looked up from her plate. "You seem to think this is some kind of democracy. That's not how these projects work, okay? Sorry. I'm the one who's in charge of assigning the jobs, and I've already decided that Deirdre, Ashley, and I can handle the decorating just fine on our own. Your job is to help Wayne and JT with the other stuff."

"Hey, what about us?" Audrey spoke up. "What are we supposed to do?"

"You three are floaters," Synndi told her. "You get to help wherever you're needed. There should be plenty of variety to keep you entertained."

"Hold on a second here." I like to think of myself as a pretty even-tempered person. But Synndi's imperious behavior was wearing on my last nerve, and I was already getting tired of hiding it. "We're all supposed to be working together on this project, remember? Hazel didn't say anything about—"

"Hazel's not here anymore." Synndi shrugged coolly. "That's why she left me in charge. You ought to be glad I'm here instead of complaining about it. I used to help my ex organize huge parties and galas all the time—I'm definitely the most experienced person here at that sort of thing."

"Yeah," Deirdre spoke up with a smirk. "What's the last gala you organized, Nancy? Backyard barbecues with your little friends don't count."

I opened my mouth to protest further, but Synndi cut me off before I could speak. "I'm finished," she announced, pushing away her empty plate. "That sauce was a little salty, Nancy. I certainly hope there's something sweet for dessert to take the edge off."

Gritting my teeth, I stood without answering and headed for the kitchen, wondering rather peevishly how someone as rail-thin as Synndi could eat so much. Grabbing a container of ice cream out of the freezer, I clutched it in both hands and took a few deep breaths, trying to let the cold surface of the carton cool my frazzled nerves. This project wasn't going to be any fun at all if I couldn't find a way to peacefully coexist with my coworkers. I wished Bess was there—she could get along with just about anybody. Even though Deirdre was far from her favorite person, Bess could usually charm her, if necessary. I was sure she could do the same with Synndi and Ashley.

Then again, if Bess were here, that would mean George would be here too, I thought with a hint of a smile. And if George were here, she would have strangled Deirdre within the first half hour, then tossed Synndi and Cousin Ashley into the river for good measure. . . .

The thought made me a little homesick for my friends, but it also made me chuckle a little. That gave me the strength to swallow down my irritation and also face the others again. I grabbed a large spoon from a drawer and headed back into the dining room.

JT had disappeared while I was in the kitchen, so I set the ice cream in front of Wayne. "Here you go," I said, forcing as much cheerfulness as I could manage into my voice. "Why don't you start this off, Wayne?"

"That's okay," Wayne said, his voice eager and overloud. "Why don't you let Synndi have the first scoop?"

I blinked at him in surprise. So far I hadn't been paying much attention to Wayne—I'd had my hands full with Synndi and her little cronies. But now I noticed that he was really rather handsome in a nerdy sort of way. He had broad shoulders, a quick smile, and nice blue eyes. And right now those eyes were trained on Synndi with an expression that could only be described as "lovesick puppy." I hid a smile as he half rose from his seat, offering the carton of ice cream in Synndi's direction.

Synndi didn't even bother to look up. "None for me, thanks. I changed my mind about dessert."

If she noticed that Wayne was still staring at her adoringly—and there was little chance she could miss it—she gave no indication of it. It didn't take a detective to deduce that Synndi's pretty, angelic face hid a selfish personality. No wonder she seemed to be bonding so quickly with Deirdre and Ashley . . .

"Okay, then." Wayne seemed undaunted by her reaction. "If you change your mind, let me know. I can scoop it out for you if it's too frozen or whatever."

"Have some pride, dude," one of the teens muttered just loudly enough for everyone at the table to hear. Her friends snickered.

48

"What was that, Licey?" Ashley demanded, shooting the girl an irritated look.

"It's Lacy," the girl retorted.

Deirdre rolled her eyes. "Whatever," she said. "Just pipe down, would you? The grown-ups are talking."

"Grown-ups?" Audrey spoke up. "What are you—like, eighteen?"

"Just be quiet, would you?" Synndi said irritably. "Hey, Wayne, why don't you take these children out to the other room and, you know, play a board game with them or something?"

"Sure, anything you say!" Wayne jumped out of his seat as the three girls snickered again. "What should we play? Monopoly? Battleship?"

I sighed, feeling a little sorry for Wayne. He was so swoon-y over Synndi that he didn't even seem to notice that the girls were laughing at him. Suddenly I was so sick of the selfish ex-beauty-queen and most of the others in the room that I didn't think I could sit there for even one more minute. Besides, I wanted to call home and see how George's teeth extraction had gone. Despite my less-than-luxurious lodgings, I was almost grateful for the chance to escape from the B and B for the night.

"Excuse me," I said, rising from the table and faking a yawn. "I think I'm going to turn in early tonight."

Ashley raised one eyebrow as she glanced at her watch. "Early is right," she said. "It's not even eight o'clock." She glanced over at Deirdre. "You weren't kidding when you said people around here go to bed early."

"Yeah." Deirdre was busy digging into the ice-cream carton. "What can I say? I told you this was the boondocks."

"Wait a second, Nancy," Synndi said. "What about the dishes? Someone has to clean up after dinner."

"You're right, someone does," I said firmly. "But that someone isn't me. Good night."

I hurried for the door before she could protest. Outside on the bed-and-breakfast's wide, wood-planked front porch, I paused and took a few deep breaths of the warm evening air. Despite the high-light of meeting Hazel Perrault, overall it had been a tiring and rather confusing first day, and I wasn't sure what to think of it. All I could do was remind myself that I was here to *help*, not necessarily to have fun—and hope that tomorrow went a little better.

Realizing it was getting dark and I didn't have a flashlight with me—where had I put my pocket flashlight?—I headed down the porch steps and across the field toward the theater. Nobody had bothered to leave the lobby lights on for me, but enough of the fading daylight trickled in through the big double doors to allow me to find my way across the debris-littered floor and into my little room. I flicked on the light switch just inside the door, bringing the single overhead bulb to life.

Sitting down on the cot, I dug my cell phone out of my duffel and clicked power. But instead of the usual cheerful chirp, it remained silent.

"Oh no," I murmured, trying to remember the last time I'd charged it. Then I switched to trying to remember if I'd packed the charger. I dug into the bag again, and breathed a sigh of relief when my hand closed around a familiar, hard, plastic object.

Glancing around the room I saw that electrical outlets were in short supply. There was one, located near the floor beside the lounge door leading into the bathroom half of my "suite."

I hurried over and blew on the outlet to chase away most of the dust and cobwebs. Then I plugged the charger's cord into the outlet. Before I could insert the phone into the charger, there was a sputtering sound, then a muffled click. A split second later the bulb overhead went out, plunging the room into darkness.

I groaned, realizing the charger must have shorted out the circuit. "God forbid anyone should try to use a blow dryer or something in here," I muttered, making a mental note to mention the problem to JT and Wayne the next day.

It was pitch-black in the windowless room, but luckily I remembered the flashlight I'd tucked into my duffel along with my work gloves and the other equipment I'd thought I might need for the project. A few minutes of blind digging turned it up. I held my breath as I clicked the switch, hoping it wouldn't turn out to be as dead as my cell phone. I couldn't have that much bad luck in one day, could I?

"Whew." I breathed aloud as a strong white beam shot out from the flashlight, illuminating the fat black spider busily spinning its web near the foot of the bed. "Now, if I were a circuit box in an old movie theater, where would I be?"

Light in hand, I ventured back out into the darkened lobby. I'd only taken a few steps, sweeping the flashlight beam over the walls in search of a basement or utility-room door, when I heard a soft *thunk* behind me. I froze, straining my ears.

"Hello?" I said softly, feeling slightly foolish at the thought that I was probably talking to a rat or something.

"Hello."

I jumped, spinning around and aiming my flashlight in the direction of the voice. The beam caught a squinting JT, who was standing near the door leading into the main theater area.

"Wha-what are you doing here?" I cried, startled by his unexpected appearance.

"Just checking on things before I head out for the night. Sorry I startled you."

"Oh." I already felt silly for my reaction. Trying to quiet my racing heart, I smiled apologetically at him. "Sorry. Guess I'm just jumpy. I accidentally shorted out the light in my room. . . ."

With JT's help, the lights were soon on again. "If you want to plug something in, use the outlets in the bathroom," he told me. "Wiring's better in there."

"Thanks."

After he left I went into the bathroom. It wasn't much bigger than the lounge area. There was just space enough for a line of three stalls facing a countertop containing three sinks. I plugged the charger into the outlet above one of the sinks and inserted the phone. It would take a couple of hours to fully charge, and by then it would be too late to make my calls. As much as I didn't feel like facing Synndi and her minions again that night, I figured I might as well suck it up and head back to the B and B to use the phone there.

Night had come over the island in earnest during my little circuit-shorting escapade, and I was happy to have my flashlight to augment the weak light of the new moon peeking out from behind the clouds. As I crossed the field at a brisk walk, I could see that the lights were already out on the first floor of the bed-and-breakfast, though most of the windows upstairs were still lit.

I quietly let myself into the house. The sitting room was empty; the only evidence of recent occupation were the embers of a fire Wayne had lit in the fireplace just before dinner. Wondering if I could possibly get away without running into anyone, I tiptoed across the room without turning on the lights. There was a phone on the end table beside the sofa, and I picked it up, already trying to figure out how to describe Synndi to my friends.

I put the phone to my ear and heard voices. Oops. Someone was already on the line on another extension. My hand was already moving to hang up the phone when I froze, my attention captured by the words coming over the line.

"And I already know the perfect way to sneak it out right under everyone's noses," a whispering female voice was saying urgently. "Now all we have to do is figure out a good way to make the switch, and all that money will be ours!"

5

Questions and Discoveries

I pressed the phone to my ear, listening intently. But the other person on the line must have heard the click when I picked up.

"Did you hear that?" a male voice whispered. "This line isn't safe."

I silently replaced the phone before I could hear any more, then scurried for the door. A few dozen yards from the house, flashlight off and feeling hidden by the darkness, I stopped and turned to look back at the house. My heart was pounding as I tried to figure out exactly what I'd just heard. Who had that been on the line? All I could tell was that one voice had been female and the other male.

And what was meant by that comment about the money? Even as I tried to recollect exactly what I'd heard, part of me knew that it could have an innocuous explanation. Maybe it was just Deirdre plotting to sweet-talk her father out of more money. Or one of the teen girls concocting some sort of scheme with a boyfriend.

But another part of me wasn't convinced. My friends say I have a nose for a mystery, a sort of sixth sense or instinct that starts pinging when something isn't quite right. And it was pinging away like crazy at the moment.

I wasn't sure what to do about it, though. Glancing around I saw that lights were still shining out from the front windows on both the second and third floor, indicating that Deirdre and Synndi, at least, were still awake. The construction workers' truck was still parked in the B and B's driveway, where it had been from the time the van dropped us off. That meant Wayne was probably still around somewhere, too.

For a moment I thought about going back inside to snoop around a little, or at least walk around to the side of the house to check for lights in the other windows. But all of a sudden the exhaustion of the day caught up with me. I needed to get back to my humble little bed before I collapsed.

Whatever mystery I'd just uncovered—if it was a mystery at all—could wait until morning.

"Look, I told you. No whispering while I'm in charge, okay?" I wiped a bead of sweat from my brow and glared at Audrey.

"What do you care if we whisper?" the girl challenged, sticking out her chin. "Why can't we do what we want?"

I sighed and leaned on the handle of my broom. "For the fifth time, because. I. Said. So." I was trying to be patient with the girls, but whatever patience I'd started out with was quickly running out. Synndi, Deirdre, and Ashley had left for town right after breakfast to shop for fabric. Don't ask me why that task required all three of them; it was just another facet of Synndi's master plan.

Meanwhile JT and Wayne were busy dismantling the bolted-down theater seats. That left me to supervise three rambunctious teens who seemed more interested in sneaking off to whisper and gossip than in sweeping the ash and dust out of the lobby and adjoining areas, which was what we were supposed to be doing according to Synndi's orders.

"Hey, you'd better watch out," Lacy warned me with a smirk. "Or we'll sic the theater ghost on you."

Meghan giggled. "Yeah. In the movies the ghosts always go after the mean people."

I rolled my eyes, biting my tongue to keep from

snapping at her. The three of them kept joking around about the theater being haunted, claiming they'd felt ghostly breezes or sensed unseen eyes watching them while they worked. I suspected they'd been up way too late the night before, swapping spooky stories.

Still, despite all their attempts to goof off, we were actually getting a lot of work done. We'd already cleaned out the projection room, and we were making good progress on the lobby. When they weren't getting on my nerves, the girls were actually sort of fun and interesting. All three of them had lived pretty tough lives so far with histories of family problems, vandalism, petty theft, and various other issues. But they were smart and funny and seemed ready for the fresh start this community center we were creating was supposed to provide for them. It made the project—even the aggravating parts of it—seem all the more worthwhile.

"Look," I said, "I'm going to start cleaning out that closet behind the snack counter. Can I count on you guys to keep sweeping and not run off somewhere?"

They all shrugged, which I decided to take as a yes. I headed for the closet, which was located at the far end of the area behind the glass-topped snack-bar counter. I'd glanced into it earlier while sweeping and noted that about three closets' worth of junk was stored in there.

Now I saw that my first impression hadn't been wrong. The closet was stuffed to the gills with all sorts of random items—old register receipts, mops and buckets, long-stale boxes of candy, dusty rolls of paper towels—shoved in together willy-nilly.

"Well, it's all gotta come out," I mumbled to myself.

Once I started digging in I realized that among the cleaning supplies and empty popcorn boxes was some interesting stuff. I found an old-fashioned manual cash register, a few rolled-up movie posters from long-ago films, a set of hand-carved wooden poles connected by velvet ropes, several anonymous film reels . . . The whole history of the old theater seemed to be contained within the closet.

I was reaching for something on the top shelf when my elbow hit a stapler, sending it flying. It fell to the bottom of the closet, bouncing off something near the back, ringing like a bell from the impact. I brushed aside some rags and papers and uncovered a large, dusty glass jug with a narrow opening at the top.

Curious I decided to drag it out into the light for a better look. That was easier said than done—the rounded surface of the jug was smooth to start with, and a slick coating of years'-old grime made it even more difficult to get a handhold. I finally managed to pull it out of the closet by wedging one hand into the narrow opening at the top of the jug to get a grip that way. My fingers almost ended up stuck in there, but I yanked them loose and then tipped the jug on its side, rolling it out from behind the counter and across the lobby into the beams of sunlight illuminating the floor just inside the wide-open front doors.

"What's that?" Meghan glanced up from her sweeping.

"I'm not sure," I said. "Looks like some kind of antique jug. I wonder what it was used for."

The jug was big—about three feet tall and two across. Its rounded body tapered smoothly to the bottleneck, which stuck up a few inches at the top and was a little too narrow for me to fit my entire hand all the way through. I was chipping at the coating of dirt on the outside, wondering if there might be any kind of identifying mark on the glass, when I heard voices chatting and laughing outside. A moment later Synndi strode into view, trailed as usual by Deirdre and Ashley.

"How's everything going in here, people?" Synndi called out cheerfully. "You'll all be glad to hear that our trip to town was wonderfully successful. We found some fantastic fabric for the curtains, and . . . Hey, what's that?"

She was staring curiously at my jug. "I'm not sure," I said. "I found it in the supply closet and brought it out here for a better look. Kind of interesting-looking, isn't it?"

I expected her to roll her eyes or say something snotty. To my surprise, she nodded and stepped closer.

"It's pretty grimy," she murmured. "But if we get it all cleaned up . . ." She glanced up at me with a pleased smile. "Good eye, Nancy. This will make the perfect container for collecting cash donations at the fund-raiser. Hazel asked me to come up with something that would work—you know, in case people want to give more once they arrived."

"Oh. Well, yeah, I guess this should work pretty well for something like that," I agreed. I suspected that Synndi was planning to take credit for my find, but I didn't really care about that. It was nice to have contributed to the cause, even anonymously. "Do you want me to try cleaning it off?"

"No, Deirdre and Ash can do that." Synndi waved a hand toward the pair, not seeming to notice their matching looks of dismay at her words. "You keep working on the cleanup. It'll be time to start dinner soon, so you don't want to get distracted."

I nodded, then turned around quickly to hide my grimace. For some reason Synndi had decided I was to remain the group's designated cook. She'd ordered me to make every meal so far. Except for that first dinner last night, I'd been expected to clean up afterward too. It was already getting old, but I wasn't sure what else to do other than do as she said. For one thing, I was still doing my best to get along, since it wouldn't do the project any favors to start a war over something so petty.

Besides, if I didn't do the cooking, I wasn't sure who could. Deirdre and Ashley probably couldn't even make toast. And the teen girls rolled their eyes at every vegetable and nutritious item I'd presented so far. I couldn't imagine what they would come up with as a meal. The two men had more to do than the rest of us, since they were responsible for all the hard-core construction work that had to be done, so it didn't seem either fair or prudent to take them away from that to cook for the rest of us. That left me and Synndi. Except according to Queen Synndi, that left . . . just me.

I tried not to let it bother me too much. Cooking wasn't my favorite activity in the world, but I didn't really mind it, either. So I didn't say a word as Synndi leaned over the jug. I just looked around the lobby. At first I couldn't see the girls anywhere, and I let out a sigh, certain that they'd crept off for another attempt at gossip.

Then I spotted them. They were clustered together at the lobby's only window, which overlooked the field between the theater and the bed-and-breakfast.

All three of them had their noses pressed against the cloudy glass, staring intently at something outside and whispering to one another.

I stepped closer. "Hey," I said when I was a few feet away. "What are you looking at?"

They immediately jumped back and spun around, looking much more guilty and sheepish than they had at any of the times I'd caught them huddled together. "Nothing," Audrey said quickly. "Just taking a break. No big."

"Oh." As they scurried away, I walked to the window and peered out. The only person in sight was JT, who was tossing some scrap metal into a Dumpster in the parking lot.

"Weird," I murmured, confused. If it had been Wayne out there, I might have assumed the girls had a crush on him or something. But JT was far too old for them to be drooling over him.

Glancing over my shoulder, I saw that the three of them were already hard at work sweeping and dusting. Whatever they'd been doing, it probably didn't mean much of anything . . . unlike certain other behaviors I'd uncovered lately. With that my mind drifted back to that mysterious phone call the night before. Yes, I definitely had more interesting things to think about than the mysterious behavior of a bunch of fourteen-year-olds. . . .

A big project is always full of surprises—things go awry at the last minute, materials fail, or people fall behind schedule. It's all just part of the game. Countless intricate parts must fit together, interlocking perfectly in order to form the whole.

The Chateau Theater project was no exception. From the late discovery of wiring problems to the unexpected quantity of ash still coating every surface inside and out, it looked doubtful for a time that the process would ever come to its desired conclusion. But neither myself nor my intrepid volunteers ever lost heart. For it's only through challenges that our will is tested, and it's the end result that really matters. . . .

6

Food for Thought

After dinner that night I finally got a chance to call home on my fully charged cell phone. I called my father first to let him know I was okay.

"So how's the project going?" he asked.

I sighed, shifting my weight to avoid a particularly lumpy spot on my cot. "Mostly okay."

"Mostly?" My father is no dummy; he could tell I wasn't as enthusiastic as I could be. "Nancy, what's going on down there?"

"I'm having trouble getting along with the woman who's sort of in charge," I admitted.

"You mean Hazel Perrault?" Dad sounded surprised. "What's the problem?"

"No, no," I corrected quickly. "Hazel's awesome. But she had to leave for most of the week because of other

65

commitments, and the person she left in charge isn't quite as awesome. Do you remember Synndi Aulnoy?"

Dad chuckled. "Who could forget her?" he said. "She's quite a character. What's she doing on a project like this? Volunteering doesn't seem up her alley."

"I don't know." I shrugged, even though I knew he couldn't see me. "But she's taken over the whole thing, and it's not pretty. She's like a drill sergeant on steroids, and I'm her favorite private."

"Well, I'm sure you'll figure out a way to—oops, hold on a sec, Nancy. That's my other line." The line went dead for a moment, then he clicked back on. "Sorry, honey, I have to take this call. Are you going to be okay?"

"Sure, I'll be fine. I'll call you in a couple of days."

I pressed the End button to hang up, then dialed George's cell number. It rang several times before there was a click as someone picked up.

"Mmm-oh?" a muffled voice answered.

"George? Is that you? It's me."

There was another mumble, then a pause. Then Bess's voice came on the line.

"Nancy? Hey, how's it going? I keep telling George to just let me answer the phone, but you know how stubborn she—ow! Hey, stop it!"

I grinned. Bess's voice was like a welcome breath of fresh air in my dank little bedroom. "Sounds like the patient is kind of feisty," I said.

"Definitely," Bess replied with a giggle. "She's more trouble than the two twelve-year-olds combined. The only good thing is that her mouth is still too sore to complain much. Unfortunately, the oral surgeon said she should be back to normal in a few days."

"That's good. I take it the surgery was a success?"

"Yeah, I guess. So how are things down there? Is Deirdre driving you crazy yet?"

"Sort of," I admitted. "And she's not the only one—have you heard of Synndi Aulnoy?"

"Of course!" Bess responded immediately. "Why? Is she part of this project too? I can't believe I couldn't go—it would've been too cool to meet her!"

"Don't be so sure," I said grimly. I went on to summarize Synndi's irritating personality, along with my cooking and cleaning duties. Bess relayed the information to George, reporting back that her mumbles sounded outraged.

"I don't really mind doing it," I went on with a sigh. "But it's pretty annoying when Synndi criticizes the food I make. She keeps saying even her boyfriend is a better cook, and he barely knows how to make cold cereal." I rolled my eyes as I thought about her comments that evening at dinner. "Of course, she spends, like, half her time bragging about her fabulous new boyfriend."

Bess chuckled. "I guess she's trying to convince herself she traded up after her divorce," she said. "Didn't Deirdre's father handle that? Synndi must be totally sucking up to her about now."

"Really? Mr. Shannon was Synndi's divorce attorney? I didn't know that; I just knew Dad turned down the case," I said. "In any case it's not really working that way. If anything, Deirdre is sucking up to Synndi. Her cousin Ashley too. They're like a pair of adoring little groupies or something. I guess they just automatically admire anyone who's even richer and thinner and more expensively dressed than they are."

I immediately felt a little guilty for such a petty thought. But Bess just laughed. "Probably," she agreed. "So aside from that, how's everything going?"

"Okay." I switched the phone to my other ear. "Well, except that there have been a few sort of . . . you know . . . odd moments here and there."

"What do you mean, 'odd moments'?"

In between playing cop all afternoon with the girls who kept gossiping instead of working, I'd had plenty of time to ponder that phone call I'd overheard, along with a few other things that had been nagging at the back of my mind. "Nothing big," I said. "But I overheard someone in the house on the phone. The conversation was all in whispers, and it was something about sneaking something out of somewhere and making a switch and money."

"Hmm. Who was on the phone?"

"I don't know." I stood up and starting pacing from one end of my room to the other. It only took about six steps each way. "All I could tell was that it was a man and a woman talking. But that's not all—at the introductory meeting yesterday, there was sort of a weird moment with Hazel Perrault. We were talking about the fund-raiser or something, and she sort of hesitated and got a funny look on her face. I'm not sure, but it sort of seemed like she switched the topic over to my detective work right then. It may have been nothing, but it was definitely odd. Plus one of the construction workers has the same last name as the Riverside arsonist. His name is Jordan T. Jefferson. Pretty weird to be a coincidence, right?"

"I guess." Bess didn't sound particularly convinced, but she dutifully repeated it all to George. "Jefferson's a pretty common name, though. And the other stuff, well . . ."

She trailed off tactfully, not saying what she was obviously thinking—that it all sounded pretty weak. "I know," I said, confirming her doubts. "But I just have a hunch that there might be something going on."

Bess laughed. "Uh-oh, a patented Nancy Drew hunch," she teased. "Are you sure spending all that time with Deirdre and her buddies isn't just making you desperate for something else to think about, like a nice juicy mystery? Not that we would blame you." She paused for a moment. "George is nodding at that, by the way."

"I know," I admitted. "It might all be a big bunch of nothing. But if George feels up to it, can you ask her to look into the name thing a little? You know, see what she can find out online about a JT Jefferson . . ."

"Sure, hold on." In the background, I could hear Bess passing on my request. Then she came back on the line. "She rolled her eyes and sort of snorted. But she said she'd try."

"Thanks." Under the circumstances that was the most I could ask for. "I'll call you guys tomorrow."

The next morning I was yanked out of a sound sleep by an annoying pain in my shoulder and the sense of someone hovering over me. I opened my eyes and blinked groggily at Synndi, who was leaning over my cot poking me with one long, thin finger.

"Rise and shine, Nancy," she said. "We have a long day ahead of us, and we'll need a good breakfast to get started."

I groaned and pushed her finger away. "All right, all right," I mumbled, too tired to argue or even complain about her method of waking me. "I'm coming."

She hurried out of the room as I sat up and glanced at my watch. At first I thought my sleep-blurred eyes were deceiving me—it couldn't really be five thirty a.m., could it?

It could. And it was.

I groaned again, mumbling a few uncomplimentary comments under my breath about Synndi and her obnoxious job assignments. But I was awake by then, so I figured I might as well get started on the day.

Breakfast was ready and waiting by the time Deirdre, Ashley, and the girls wandered downstairs around seven. I'd already eaten, so Synndi sent me over to get started at the theater. I was using a scythe to chop down some of the tall weeds in the overgrown yard when the men arrived a few minutes later.

"Where's Synndi?" Wayne asked eagerly as soon as he hopped out of JT's truck.

I wiped the sweat off my brow with the back of one hand and glanced at him. "Over at the house," I said wearily. "Making up more chores for the rest of us to do."

Wayne laughed uncertainly as if he wasn't sure whether I was joking or not. "Oh, okay," he said. "Guess we'll just get started, then . . ."

He turned and hurried after JT, who was already heading for the door in his usual silent fashion. I leaned on the handle of my scythe for a moment, resting and staring after the older man. My friends thought I was making up mysteries when none existed. Were they right? Or could JT possibly have some connection to the Riverside arsonist? And even if he did, what did it mean? Could he have been the male voice on the phone the other night?

Just then I spotted Synndi marching across the fields with the three teenagers behind her. I quickly hoisted my scythe and got back to work on the weeds.

"Lunch is here!" Synndi announced cheerfully from the direction of the front yard.

At the word *lunch*, my stomach let out an audible growl. We'd all spent the past few hours hard at work. Once I'd finished with the weeds out front, I'd tackled the grimy floors of the main theater. The men had removed all the seats from the front half of the room the day before, so I was able to mop and scrub in preparation for putting down new flooring. It was satisfying work, but difficult and exhausting as well, and I was more than ready for a break.

I ran into Deirdre in the lobby on my way to answer Synndi's call. "Does this mean someone else cooked for a change?" I wondered aloud.

She shot me a snotty look. "Don't be stupid," she said. "Synndi ordered sandwiches. No offense, but we're all getting a little sick of your so-called cooking."

I rolled my eyes and ignored the comment. It wasn't even worth the energy to respond. "Sandwiches sound great," I said. "I could eat about three right now."

Synndi was on the front lawn passing out food when I reached her. "There you go, Audrey—chicken salad with no crust, just like you ordered," she was saying. "Oh, Deirdre, there you are. I have your seared tuna wrap right here."

"Good. I'm starved." Deirdre reached for the sandwich Synndi had just pulled out of a bag printed with the logo of a local deli.

When she looked up to hand it to her, Synndi spotted me and blinked. "Oh, dear," she said. "Nancy. I knew I forgot someone. . . ."

"Huh?" I said, hungrily eyeing the large, mostly empty deli bag.

She shrugged elaborately. "I guess I counted wrong when I was taking the lunch orders," she said, her voice sickly sweet. "It seems I completely forgot to order you a sandwich at all. So I'm afraid there's nothing here for you."

I just stared at her for a moment. Maybe it was the overwhelming hunger, but for a second I really didn't understand. "You mean I don't get any lunch?" I asked in disbelief.

"There were plenty of leftovers from those gross pancakes you forced us to eat this morning for breakfast," Ashley spoke up as she carefully laid out her grilled vegetable wrap on her lap. "Maybe you can eat that."

I glared at her. "Very funny," I said, fed up—no pun intended—with the terrible trio's snarky little comments. "Maybe if someone else would volunteer to cook once in a while . . ."

"Look, Nancy, there's no need to get snippy," Synndi broke in sanctimoniously. "Accidents happen, and I've already apologized. So you might as well head back to the house and find yourself something to eat instead of taking it out on us."

"Yeah," Deirdre piped in with a smirk.

"No need for that."

The gruff male voice took us all by surprise. JT spoke so seldomly that I think it always startled the rest of us a little when he did. I turned to see him breaking his large submarine sandwich in half.

"Here you go, young lady," he said, holding it out to me. "You can share mine. Hope you like roast beef."

"Sure," I blurted, so taken aback by the unexpected gesture that I wasn't sure how to react. "I love roast beef. Thanks."

Deirdre and Ashley rolled their eyes at each other,

and Synndi just shrugged. That seemed to be the end of that.

For the next half hour I sat in the shade that was cast by the building, enjoying the hearty sandwich and the chance to rest. I also listened as Synndi, Ashley, Deirdre, and Wayne discussed their decorating plans while they ate. The three younger girls were sunbathing on the grass nearby, paying no attention to any of us as they talked and giggled among themselves. JT had gulped down his food quickly, then disappeared back into the theater.

"According to my schedule, if we all keep working hard we'll definitely be done in plenty of time," Synndi said as she crumpled up the wrapper from her sandwich. "Maybe we'll even have a few extra hours to get ready for the fund-raising party."

"Cool," Deirdre said eagerly. "If I'm going to meet Jake Perrault, I definitely want to look my best!"

Ashley wrinkled her nose. "Don't bother," she said confidently. "As soon as Jake lays eyes on me, he'll be totally in love. The rest of you won't even be on his radar."

"Whatever," Deirdre said with a giggle. "I hope you'll let me be in your wedding, at least. That way I can meet all his movie-star friends."

"No problem," Ashley replied generously. "You can be my maid of honor."

Synndi just rolled her eyes. But I couldn't resist

speaking up. After all the obnoxious things Ashley had said to me over the past two days, it was just too tempting to tease her a little.

"Don't be too sure about that, Ashley," I said with mock seriousness. "Some others of us might have our sights set on Jake too."

"Yeah, right," Deirdre said with a snort.

Ashley turned to glare at me. "Very funny, Nancy," she snapped. "As if Jake would ever be interested in someone like *you*."

"Don't be so sure." I waggled my eyebrows suggestively. "I clean up better than you might think. And Jake's mother already likes me—that might give me the edge I need to land him."

"Shut up!" Ashley cried, her cheeks going red. "You'd better not get in my way, or you'll be sorry!"

She looked so upset that I was sorry for starting with her. I opened my mouth to admit I was just kidding around. But Synndi spoke up first.

"Enough, Nancy," she said sternly. "Quit trying to stir up trouble. It's not very mature. If you're so bored that that's all you can think of to do, maybe it's time to get back to work. You can start by clearing out the area behind the old movie screen. It's a mess back there."

"Yeah," Ashley snapped. "A mess—just like your dreams of ever getting a guy like Jake to even look at you."

I was more than a little tempted to tell Synndi exactly where she could stick her orders. But I bit my tongue, reminding myself for the umpteenth time that I was here to help. I could put up with much worse than Synndi, Ashley, and Deirdre for such a good cause.

So I kept quiet, merely rolling my eyes at the ridiculousness of the whole conversation as I got up and went inside to do as Synndi said. I'd noticed the grungy piles of ash, dirt, and trash behind the screen too, and I figured it was time to tackle it.

When I got back there, I found that one of the overhead lights had burned out, leaving the narrow, musty area dim and shadowy. Once I'd pushed past the heavy, dusty velvet stage curtain and then the edge of the stiff movie screen, I had to squint to see more than a few feet in front of me.

As I started sweeping up the nearest pile of ash, there was a sudden, faint rustling noise in one corner. I paused in midsweep, my heart pounding a little faster as I tried to pinpoint the source. It was kind of spooky back there in the near-dark, cut off from the rest of the theater by the huge pale expanse of the screen and the sound-muffling curtains.

It came again—a sort of skittering sound as if the crumpled paper cups and scraps of newspaper were coming to life in the shadowy corners. I wet my lips, suddenly more nervous than I liked to admit. Warning myself not to freak out over nothing, I took a cautious step toward the source of the sound. The younger girls' talk of ghosts popped into my mind, and I shook my head in irritation. The creepy atmosphere was getting to me a little, and I didn't like it.

Rustle. Rustle. This time I saw definite movement in one of the piles of paper scraps. I leaned forward, squinting against the darkness . . . and jumped back, startled, as a tiny grayish figure suddenly zoomed out and across the room.

I laughed, surprised by how relieved I was to recognize the fast-moving little shape. "A mouse," I murmured. "Duh." It wasn't the first time I'd caught a glimpse of one of the furry little creatures in the theater. In fact, I was pretty sure I'd spotted one peering at me from the foot of my cot late the night before. But mice didn't scare me. Under the circumstances they almost seemed like friendly visitors.

Taking a deep breath to clear my head, I focused once again on my task, banishing all thoughts of ghostly intruders. I squatted down to brush the mouse-chewed pile of papers into my dustpan.

There was another, louder rustling sound from nearby. I glanced up just in time to see a shadowy figure, much bigger than a mouse, lunge out from behind the screen and loom over me.

7

Suspicions and Surprises

I screamed at the top of my lungs and leaped to my feet, sending the contents of my dustpan flying everywhere.

"Whoa!" a familiar gruff voice said. "Settle down, miss. It's just me."

"JT?" I stared at him, my panic subsiding into embarrassment. "Um, sorry for screaming like that. You just startled me, that's all."

"Sorry." JT shrugged. "Didn't mean to."

"It's okay."

But I wasn't quite ready to let it go. Despite his nice gesture with the sandwich earlier, I still wasn't quite sure what to think about JT. There was something about him . . . something just a bit too silent and mysterious, especially compared with the chatterboxes that made up the rest of our little group. Was he really just here to help out and do a good deed, or was there something else going on behind those quiet gray eyes of his?

"Synndi is looking for you," JT said as I stared at him thoughtfully. "She's got a job for you outside when you're finished in here."

"Thanks." I brushed off my knees and then bent to pick up the dustpan I'd dropped. "So, JT, we haven't really had a chance to talk. Are you originally from around here?"

"Yup." He didn't seem inclined to elaborate any further.

"That's nice." I tried to think of a polite way to phrase my next question. "Um, so how did you come to be a part of this little project?"

He shrugged. "Seemed like a worthy cause."

"Yeah, me too," I agreed. He was already turning to leave, but I wasn't quite ready to let him go yet. "So you must have been around town at the time the Riverside arsonist was doing his thing, huh?"

He stopped short, glancing back at me. "No," he said shortly. "As a matter of fact, I wasn't."

"Really? Why not?"

"Did anybody ever tell you that you ask a lot of questions?" he asked with a growl. With that he stalked out of the room, muttering something

I couldn't quite hear under his breath.

Interesting. I couldn't tell if he'd been trying to evade my question or was just annoyed to *be* questioned, but it was the biggest reaction to anything I'd seen from him so far.

I headed outside to find out what Synndi wanted. She was shouting instructions at Wayne as he stacked lumber. Despite the way she ordered him—and the rest of us—around, his crush on her didn't appear to have abated. He seemed willing to do anything she ordered, no matter how menial or capricious. It only proved there was no accounting for taste. . . .

Synndi spotted me approaching. "There you are," she said sourly. "Took you long enough to get here. Listen, forget about the stuff inside for now. Ashley just heard on the radio that it might rain tomorrow. So you'd better sweep up the piles of ash and stuff in the back parking lot."

"Okay, whatever." I wasn't really looking forward to going back into that dark little area behind the screen anyway.

Then again, I'd seen the back parking lot. It looked like the surface of the moon. Most of the ash and soot from the entire island seemed to have blown into the lot and stopped by the back wall of the building. They now formed peaks and valleys of dirty black gunk. Cleaning it up definitely wasn't a job for one person.

If I wanted to get anywhere near finished before it was time for me to start fixing dinner, I needed help. I knew better than to ask Deirdre and Ashley to pitch in—they still hadn't gotten over the strenuous task of cleaning out that glass jug the day before, though surprisingly they'd done a pretty good job.

I glanced around. JT was nowhere in sight, and Wayne was still busy being ordered around by Synndi. That left the three younger girls. The last time I'd seen them, they were scraping old paint off the walls of the projection room. Figuring they were probably ready for some fresh air by now, I decided to enlist their help.

Finding them turned out to be harder than expected. When I reached the projection room, I found the paint-scraping equipment abandoned and no sign of the girls anywhere.

"Uh-oh," I murmured, images of procrastinating girls dancing through my mind.

I headed back outside. As soon as I rounded the back corner of the building, I spotted them. The three girls were huddled together in the grassy area a short distance beyond the edge of the parking lot. They appeared to be passing something around among themselves, but I couldn't see what it was. My first thought was that they were sharing a cigarette, but there was no sign of smoke. I sighed, relieved.

Stepping over a cement parking bumper and hunching down behind a scraggly bush at the edge of the parking lot, I tried to hold back a twinge of suspicion. I'd been trying not to assume the girls were up to no good all the time just because of their troubled past. But their antics so far weren't giving me that much reason to trust them, either.

As I watched, Meghan peeled away from the other two and rushed off toward the building, passing within a few yards of me without noticing me. She disappeared a second later through the back door.

Audrey and Lacy turned and walked more slowly in my direction. Not wanting them to catch me spying, I quickly jumped back, planning to wait for them around the corner of the building.

But I never got that far. I'd forgotten all about the cement bumper half hidden in the ash pile right behind me. My foot caught it as I stepped back, sending me flying backward into the parking lot—right into one of the biggest piles of ash and soot.

A huge black cloud billowed up around me as I landed flat on my back with a *whoomp*. I squeezed my eyes shut just in time to avoid the flying soot. Coughing at the explosion of dusty, smoky-smelling particles, I covered my face with my hands and struggled to sit up.

As I did I heard giggles from very close by. "Check

83

it out," Lacy cried. "Nancy's been out in the sun too long—she's got a wicked tan!"

Audrey stifled a laugh.

I carefully opened one eye just enough to squint at them. "Very funny," I said with a cough. "Mind helping me out over here?"

They each reached down and grabbed one of my arms, dragging me to my feet. Then I looked down at myself, still coughing. I was covered from head to toe with soot. My T-shirt, shorts, socks, and sneakers were all a dingy shade of ashy gray—not to mention my skin. I could only imagine what my face and hair looked like.

The younger girls were still grinning at me, seeming quite amused at my condition. "Oh well," I said weakly, realizing I couldn't blame them—I looked ridiculous. "At least maybe this way Synndi will believe I've been working hard."

Audrey let out a loud snort. "Synndi's one to talk," she said. "Ain't like she does anything around here except order us around."

"Yeah." Lacy rolled her eyes. "Especially us—and you." She nodded toward me. "It's like she hates you or something."

"Yeah, I know." I smiled at them, suddenly liking them more than I had a few seconds ago. "So what do you say—will you guys help me out? I'm supposed to be cleaning up this parking lot."

They glanced at each other and shrugged. "Sure," Audrey answered for both of them.

"Good. So where's Meghan? Maybe she can help too."

Lacy's eyes widened as she glanced quickly toward the theater. "She's, um . . . busy," she offered. "I'm sure she'll be back soon, though."

"Yeah." Audrey smirked. "She wouldn't want to miss cleaning up all these *ashes*."

Lacy grinned at her friend. "Yeah. Totally."

They were obviously sharing some kind of inside joke, which suddenly made me feel very left out and old. But I shook it off. We had work to do.

A few hours later the parking lot looked a lot better. Leaving the girls—including Meghan, who'd showed up a few minutes after we started—behind to keep working, I dragged my exhausted self across the field to the B and B to start dinner.

My sneakers left sooty prints on the clean floorboards of the porch, and I realized I needed to get myself cleaned up before I did anything else. I knew Synndi would probably want me to use the sink in the theater bathroom to wash up, but I was feeling rebellious. I figured the others probably wouldn't be back to the house for at least half an hour. That left me plenty of time to sneak upstairs to one of the bathrooms and have myself a nice, hot shower.

The second-floor bathroom shared by Deirdre, Ashley, and the younger girls was a mess—damp, makeup-stained towels hung over every available surface; toiletries and cosmetics were scattered across the countertop; and the floor was littered with clothes as well as more towels. I decided to keep going.

Synndi's third-floor suite included a spacious bathroom with a separate tub and shower. I shook my head, thinking how ridiculous it was that she had that whole place to herself while the other five people in the house were crowded into the smaller bathroom downstairs. Then again when I thought about my own humble lodgings, I couldn't feel *too* sorry for any of them.

I relaxed as the water hit the tired muscles of my back, enjoying the clouds of steam rising around me. It felt good to rinse the ash and grime off me and spiral down the drain. After scrubbing myself from head to toe, I borrowed a tiny dab of Synndi's shampoo to wash my hair.

Feeling refreshed I stepped out of the shower and checked my watch, which I'd left on the countertop. It was time to get a move on if I didn't want to be caught. I hated to put my ashy clothes back on, but I didn't have much choice. I was pretty sure Synndi would notice if I borrowed one of her fancy designer outfits, especially since it would be about four sizes too tall and three sizes too tight. So I shook my shirt and shorts out the window, doing my best to get most of the dirt off. It would have to do for now.

Once dressed I did my best to cover my tracks. I used a towel to wipe away the ashy handprints I'd left on the doorknob and shower door, and my wet footprints. As I reached for a stray sooty spot on the mirror, I noticed a small pile of receipts and loose pieces of paper on the counter. A business card sticking out of the pile looked oddly familiar, and a closer look showed why. It was Deirdre's father's distinctive burgundy, gray, and white card, which I'd seen many times.

I picked up the card and stared at it. "I guess Bess was right, then," I murmured, remembering her comment about Mr. Shannon handling Synndi's divorce.

Just then, the phone rang in the next room. Since nobody else was in the house, I hurried to answer it.

"Hello there," a cheerful voice said when I picked up. "It's Hazel. Who's this?"

"Oh! Hi, Hazel. This is Nancy."

"Nancy! How are you, my dear? I was just calling to see how everything is going. Are you having fun with the project?"

I hesitated, not sure how to respond. To answer her

question honestly, I would have to complain about how Synndi was acting like a tyrant, though I would hate to sound like a whiner.

Then there was that mysterious phone call. If my hunch was right, and there was some funny business brewing at the bed-and-breakfast, shouldn't I warn Hazel about it? Then again, what would I say? I wasn't even sure yet myself if there was anything to it. Besides, as improbable as it might seem, what if Hazel herself was the female voice on the phone? I hated to think she might be involved in something shady, but I'd learned long ago that the least likely suspect sometimes did turn out to be the culprit.

So I just said something vague about the project going well so far. Hazel asked a few more specific questions about the construction and decorating plans, which I answered as best as I could. Then she cleared her throat and paused.

"Are the others with you?" she asked. "The other volunteers, I mean."

"No. They're still at the theater. Why? Did you need to talk to someone?"

"No, no, nothing like that. I was just wondering . . ." She paused again, so long this time that for a second I thought we'd been cut off. "I just wondered what you thought of them, Nancy."

Once again I wasn't sure what to say. Something

about Hazel's tone made me think it wasn't just a casual question. "Oh, I don't know," I said as nonchalantly as I could. "They seem fine. Was there someone in particular you wanted to hear about?"

"Oh, no," she answered quickly. "I was just curious. You're probably an excellent judge of character, being such a talented sleuth. I'd enjoy hearing your impressions of anyone."

"Sure, I'd love to tell you what I think," I said. "Who should I start with?"

"Whoever pops into mind first," she replied.

We were going in circles, and I suspected we both knew it. That made me more certain than ever that there was more to Hazel's curiosity than she was letting on. Feeling a bit frustrated, I was trying to figure out a way to make her open up when there was a beeping sound.

"Oops," Hazel said. "That's my other line. I'm afraid I have to go. I'll try to call again later—perhaps we can talk more then."

After hanging up I sat there for a moment, staring at the phone. I was convinced that something was going on now. But what?

I picked up the phone again and dialed George's number, but there was no answer. Hanging up I tried Ned. He picked up on the second ring.

"Hey!" he exclaimed when he heard my voice.

"I was hoping you'd call. Having fun being a do-gooder?"

"Sort of. I'll have to fill you in later, though—I don't have much time. Do you know where George is? I asked her to look into something for me, and I need to know what she found out."

"Oh, is this about the Riverside arsonist's name thing?" he said. "I don't know where she is right now, but I spoke to her a couple of hours ago."

"Did she tell you what she found?"

"Yeah," Ned replied. "She Googled the name JT Jefferson just like you asked. There's only one person who's around the right age with that name, living in the Tributary Falls area. And get this—he just got out of prison, like, six months ago."

I gasped. "Really?"

"Wait, that's not all. She also found out that JT Jefferson is the Riverside arsonist's uncle."

While scientists and philosophers can spend lifetimes arguing about nature versus nurture, I myself am constantly amazed and amused at the ways people are shaped by their experiences—for better or for worse—and often in quite surprising ways. One ordinary person can take a difficult youth and use his or her hardships as the inspiration to grow stronger, more principled, kinder. Another can emerge from the same type of situation and use his or her past as an excuse to mistreat others . . . or, perhaps, to burn down houses. Why? Despite all those scientists' lengthy treatises on the matter, I believe that, still, no one really knows. Perhaps it goes back to the subject of my earlier musings—Fate, Luck, Chance. Perhaps it involves some sort of inherited family trait, similar to the genes for blue eyes or long legs. Or perhaps it's merely that each human on Earth is born an individual, and a leopard doesn't, after all, change its spots. . . .

8

Does Not Compute

I **was stunned by** the revelation. All this time, somehow, I'd convinced myself that JT's name was just a coincidence, a red herring that could only get in the way of whatever the real mystery might be. But now . . .

When I pressed Ned for more details he couldn't provide much information. "Sorry," he said. "George still isn't talking too well because of her teeth. And she was in kind of a grumpy mood when I talked to her."

"That's okay." I was already distracted, my mind trying to fit puzzle pieces together, make connections. "Maybe I can look into it a little more here. There's a computer downstairs."

We said good-bye, and I hurried down into the computer alcove off the sitting room. I hadn't spent much time in there, since I was usually busy in the kitchen. Now I found that it contained not only a computer, but also a fax machine, a fancy printer, a scanner, and all sorts of other bells and whistles. It wasn't at all out-of-date. As I booted up the computer I was vaguely aware that someone had entered the house, but I stayed where I was, hoping the others would leave me alone for a few more minutes. I was just logging onto the Internet when Synndi burst into the room, her face red.

"What were you doing in my room?" she demanded angrily. "I know you were in there; you made a huge mess of the place. Did you take anything?"

Oops. Belatedly I remembered that mirror smudge that I'd never quite finished cleaning up. And I'd been so distracted by Mr. Shannon's card, and then by Hazel's phone call, that I hadn't really finished checking for other signs of my presence.

"Sorry," I said, deciding to come clean, so to speak. "I just popped in to use your shower—didn't want to drop ash in everybody's dinner."

I chuckled apologetically, but Synndi didn't crack a smile. She was still glaring at me suspiciously. "Are you sure that's really what you were doing? I heard you think you're some kind of detective—you weren't snooping around or something stupid like that?"

I was surprised by how upset she seemed. Obviously she'd heard about my reputation, probably from

Deirdre. But even so, why would she be so freaked out that I'd been in her room—unless, of course, she had something to hide?

"Nope, nothing like that," I assured her mildly. "The only thing I was after was your hot water. See?"

I patted my head. Synndi blinked, focusing on my still-damp hair. I guess that convinced her I was telling the truth, because her shoulders suddenly relaxed and she shrugged.

"Oh. Okay, whatever," she muttered. "You know, most people ask permission before they go barging into other peoples' private space. Anyway, shouldn't you be cooking dinner by now?"

"Sure." It was really kind of amazing how Synndi's little bit of power had gone to her head. I couldn't help wondering if she bossed around her fabulous new boyfriend as much as she did all of us. If so, I had a hunch that the relationship might be headed for the same end as her marriage to Mr. Real Estate . . .

As Synndi stomped out of the room, I switched off the computer, realizing my research would have to wait. Then I headed into the kitchen to start dinner.

The next morning I planned to keep a close eye on JT and also observe Synndi, Wayne, and the teen girls for any suspicious comments or behavior. The week was going fast, and I needed to figure out what was going on.

Unfortunately, Synndi had other plans for me. We were all sitting around the table finishing breakfast. Ashley was picking at the French toast I'd made, wrinkling her nose and making snide little comments about it. She'd been acting noticeably cooler toward me ever since our ridiculous "fight" about Jake Perrault the day before. I'd tried to apologize a couple of times, but she'd been so childish in return that finally I'd just given up. I didn't really care if she wanted to hold a grudge about something so stupid; what could she do about it?

Little did I know.

"You know, this whole house is a total sty," she spoke up suddenly, pushing her plate away and glancing around the room with an expression of disgust. "Synndi, don't you think maybe someone should clean it up today?" She waggled her eyebrows in my general direction as she said it.

Synndi glanced from her to me. "Excellent idea, Ash," she said. "Let's see, who should do it? Hmm . . . Nancy, I think you're the best person for the job. You can stay here at the house today—you should be able to get it cleaned up by the time the rest of us get back for dinner."

"Good call, Synndi," Deirdre put in smugly, glancing up from her cereal. "After all, Nancy made most of the mess with all her cooking and stuff."

My jaw dropped at the outrageousness of that comment, not to mention the unfairness of Synndi's latest decree. "What?" I cried. "But the kitchen is the cleanest room in the house! Anyway, don't you think working at the theater would be a better use of my time? I mean, we still have tons of work to do over there before the deadline." Even as I protested, I knew it wouldn't do any good. "Maybe if you could all just clean up after yourselves . . ." I added weakly.

"Now, now, Nancy." Synndi made a little *tut-tut* noise with her tongue. "You're making a fool of yourself, sweetie. Can't you at least *try* to be a team player?"

I gritted my teeth. For a moment her condescending comment felt like that proverbial last straw, teetering on the camel's back of my tolerance for the whole situation. For a moment I was ready to get up and walk out, wash my hands of the whole project, and leave Queen Synndi and her willing little covey of admirers to try to finish on time without me.

But I took a few deep breaths and held my tongue. Maybe cleaning up after a bunch of spoiled princesses wasn't why I'd signed up for this project. But it needed to be done, and nobody else was likely to do it. Hazel was the one who would get in trouble if the others trashed the B and B, and I didn't want that to happen.

Besides, I was pretty sure it wouldn't really take me all day to get the place spick-and-span. If I finished cleaning by lunchtime, that still left me the whole afternoon to work at the theater. Most of the cleaning and construction work was finished, so that meant it was almost time for the fun part—painting, decorating, moving in the new furniture, and turning the place into a real home away from home for Audrey, Lacy, Meghan, and other girls like them. Thinking about that made me feel much better. As soon as the others left, I threw myself into the work. I didn't have to do much housework at home, aside from keeping my room neat and setting the table now and then. Dad and I mostly counted on our long-time housekeeper, Hannah Gruen, to take care of the rest, though we did our best to pitch in whenever we could. Now that I had a whole house to clean all by myself, I found it was actually kind of satisfying work. Well, except for the truly disgusting parts, like tossing Ashley's half-eaten containers of yogurt or picking Deirdre's lipstick-stained tissues out of the wad of damp towels on her floor.

When the two other rooms were clean, I dragged the vacuum down the hall to the River Room. The younger girls weren't much neater than the older ones. Remembering their sometimes odd behavior over the past couple of days, I kept a lookout for anything unusual as I cleaned. While I was trying to be careful not to accuse them of anything only because of their past, I didn't want to excuse them because of it, either. But aside from finding a couple of hand-decorated old, empty matchboxes—maybe used for jewelry?—and a few candy wrappers under a pillow, nothing in the room seemed out of place.

What was I expecting to find, anyway? I asked myself as I glanced around the room one last time. A suitcase full of unmarked cash? Automatic weapons? Passports with fake names?

I sighed, realizing I still had no idea what this mystery—if there was one—was even all about. Maybe my friends were right; maybe I was just making it all up, desperately looking for something interesting to distract me from the drudgery of being Synndi's unpaid servant.

That reminded me; I still had work to do if I wanted to get over to the theater by lunchtime. I tossed the girls' wrappers in the trash and then headed upstairs, steeling myself for another big mess. But when I reached the top of the steps, I found the door to the Sunrise Suite locked tight. I tried it again, surprised.

"Nice," I muttered, certain that my sneaky shower had something to do with this turn of events. Synndi's reaction seemed a little over-the-top and suspicious . . . or maybe just mean-spirited. Either way, it seemed I wasn't getting into her room that day. Oh well. That just meant she'd have to clean it up herself.

I headed back to the first floor. The kitchen and dining room were already pretty clean, so after loading the breakfast dishes into the dishwasher and turning it on, I headed out to the sitting room. The others had left so much junk all over the room that I soon resorted to dragging a black plastic garbage bag behind me as I vacuumed and dusted. I found candy bar wrappers on the coffee table, somebody's dirty sock under the sofa, and even an empty soda can in the ashes of the fireplace. By the time the room looked decent again, my garbage bag was more than half full.

That left the powder room, the computer room, and a couple of smaller rooms at the back of the house. I tackled the powder room first, then moved on to the computer alcove. I'd noticed during my earlier visit that there were crumpled papers all over the floor and the wastebasket was full to overflowing, so I brought my garbage bag in with me.

"Almost done," I muttered aloud, glancing around the small room. The satisfying part of my cleaning task had already worn off, and I was itching to get back to work on the theater.

Why did I let myself get stuck with all this work, anyway? I wondered as I automatically started dusting grubby fingerprints off the computer keyboard and surrounding surfaces. I'm not usually such a pushover.

It's not just cleaning up today, either. It's everything—cooking all the meals, doing exactly what Synndi says, and especially sleeping in the ladies' lounge. It's kind of crazy now that I think about it. I'm not their servant—I'm supposed to be their fellow volunteer!

Feeling sorry for myself, I dropped the paper towel I was using into the garbage bag and then leaned down to grab the wastebasket. I paused just before tipping it into the bag, surprised to see that it appeared to be full of crumpled-up pieces of plain white computer paper.

"What a waste," I murmured as I stared at it. Who would toss so much perfectly good paper away? Was it Deirdre, looking for the perfect sheet to print out those minutes for Synndi the other day?

Or maybe they did it on purpose, I thought with another flash of self-pity. Filled the wastebasket to the brim just to create even more work for me . . .

Almost immediately I shook my head, realizing I was getting a little too melodramatic about my situation. It was unlikely anyone from the brain trust at the bed-and-breakfast would think of such a thing. On the other hand, it wasn't at all hard to believe that any of the terrible trio—Synndi, Deirdre, Ashley—could be just that wasteful.

I upended the wastebasket, dumping its contents. The bits of paper tumbled out and into the garbage bag, mixing with the trash already inside. I salvaged as much paper as I could for recycling, and shook the wastebasket to make sure everything came out.

Suddenly, as the last clump of papers poured out, a flash of color caught my eye among all the white. I blinked, wondering if I'd imagined it.

Even if I didn't, who cares? I thought dully. It's probably just the spot where Deirdre was testing her new Baja Blue toenail polish. And I still have to finish this room and the rest of the first floor before I can get out of here. I don't have time to go digging around in the trash.

But I couldn't resist the twinge of curiosity. It probably didn't have anything to do with anything. Still, the detective in me couldn't let it go without taking another look.

Sitting down on the floor, I dug into the garbage bag. It was disgusting work—I'd forgotten just how many wads of chewed gum and used tea bags I'd already tossed in there. For a while I thought I'd imagined that flash of blue. Every piece of paper I uncrumpled was the same—plain white.

But finally I found it. "Aha," I murmured as I straightened out the paper on my lap.

I stared at it, not sure what I was looking at for a moment. Right in the center of the sheet was the printed image of a dollar bill. It was a bit blurry around the edges, but it was life-size and otherwise realistic in every detail except one: It was printed with blue ink rather than green ink.

"Weird," I mumbled. "If someone in the house is trying to become a counterfeiter, they're not doing a very good job...."

Just then I heard a sudden muffled commotion of screams and shouting. It sounded like it was coming from outside, in the direction of the theater. Dropping the paper back into the trash—I'd get it later—I hurried out to the front door.

As soon as I looked outside, I gasped in horror. The theater was on fire!

9

Where There's Smoke . . .

I raced across the porch, leaping down the four steps in a single bound, and took off across the field. Thick, black smoke was pouring from the lobby window, and I could still hear screams and shouts coming from inside the theater. As I got closer, I saw Deirdre and Ashley running around in the yard in front of the building, shrieking and acting generally useless—and Meghan was standing off to the side, looking worried. My heart pounded as I wondered who might still be trapped inside.

I also wondered if I should have alerted somebody—Hazel, Synndi, the local police?—when I'd found out JT was related to the Riverside arsonist. I knew I'd never forgive myself if anyone was injured and I could have prevented it.

Doing my best to push such thoughts aside, I put on a burst of speed. "What happened?" I shouted when I got close enough to the others.

"Fire! Fire!" Ashley screamed.

"I can see that," I said with as much patience as I could manage. "Did someone call 9-1-1?"

Deirdre waved her cell phone. "I called!" she cried, sounding on the verge of hysteria. "But they'll never get here in time! The stupid bridge is out, remember? We're doomed!"

I realized she had a point. There was no telling how long it would be until a fire truck could get there. That meant it was up to us. Coughing as the smoke poured into my lungs, I rushed past the pair and headed into the lobby.

The lights were still on in there, which seemed like a good sign. Following the sounds of shouting, I headed into the main theater area.

There, I saw JT and Wayne hard at work beating back the flames that were eating their way up the heavy stage curtain. Lacy and Audrey were rushing toward the men, carrying buckets sloshing over with water. I didn't realize Synndi was in the room until I heard her cough and yell out "Higher! It's getting away from you!" Glancing over, I saw her standing just inside the doorway with both long, slender arms wrapped around herself and a look of horror on her face.

I raced down to help, realizing that the fire wasn't as bad as the smoke made it look. The flames were leaping dramatically as they ate through the ancient fabric, but so far they were confined to the lower half of one side of the curtain and a small section of the carpet nearby. If we could stop them there . . .

"Girls!" I shouted, reaching the front at the same time as Audrey and Lacy. "Give the water to the guys and help me with this!" I gestured to the flames licking at the carpet, which appeared to be gaining strength.

My eyes watering from the heat and smoke, I ground my shoe onto one of the smoldering spots on the rug. Beside me, I could hear the girls coughing as they stomped at other tendrils of flame. We must have looked like a bunch of weird, avant-garde dancers hopping around in the haze of the smoke.

For a long moment, I thought it wasn't going to work—the fire continued to gain strength, both on the curtain and on the ground. But then JT scored a direct hit on the strongest part of the fire with one of the buckets. It sizzled angrily, sending steam everywhere. He and Wayne attacked the curtain with renewed vigor, beating it with their shirts and an old drop cloth until every spark was gone.

At the same time, the girls and I were making headway against the carpet fires. I could feel the heat burning through the soles of my sneakers, but I kept at it. Once the men joined us, we soon had that part of the fire out as well.

"Whew!" I said in a shaky voice when it was all over. "That was pretty scary. What happened?"

Before anyone could answer, Synndi came storming down toward us. "Thank goodness!" she exclaimed, sounding more angry than relieved. "Now would someone like to explain how this fire got started?"

Audrey shrugged. "It has something to do with oxygen, fuel, and heat. We learned that in science class."

"Very funny." Synndi crossed her arms over her chest and glared at the girl for a second before turning her suspicious gaze on the rest of us. "I think we'd better all go out and get some fresh air and get to the bottom of this."

I couldn't help agreeing with her about the fresh air. My lungs were burning, and there was an annoying tickle in my throat that was making me cough. And as much as I hated to admit it, the whole situation did seem kind of suspicious. Sure, accidents happened, fires started. But what were the odds that this particular theater, once the victim of the Riverside arsonist, would just spontaneously go up in flames again?

Once we got outside, Synndi didn't waste any time. "Okay, people," she snapped, her hands on her skinny hips. "Fires don't usually start themselves. So who did it?"

I winced. That wasn't the way I would have gone about investigating the fire myself, but I hung back to see what the response would be.

I didn't have long to wait. "She did it!" Ashley shrieked melodramatically. "It was her!"

To my surprise, when I turned to look at her, I found her pointing at me. "Huh?" I said blankly. "How could *I* have done it? I wasn't even here."

"I don't know." Ashley narrowed her eyes at me. "But you've had it in for me ever since you found out I was interested in Jake Perrault. I never thought you'd try to burn me alive, though!"

Synndi just shook her head at that, and even Deirdre rolled her eyes. "Chill, Ash," she muttered. "The smoke must be going to your head."

Glad to see that Deirdre was acting as the voice of reason for once, I turned to Wayne. "So what happened, anyway?" I asked him. "Who first discovered the fire?"

"I was helping Synndi carry those rolls of carpet inside when we smelled smoke," Wayne replied. "We followed the smell to the theater and found JT and one of those girls already in there trying to beat it out." He waved a vague hand in the direction of Audrey and Lacy, who were sitting on the grass nearby bemoaning the charred state of their shoes.

I walked over to them. "Which one of you guys

got to the fire first?" I asked, trying to keep my voice casual. "We're trying to figure out how it started."

The pair glanced at each other and shrugged in unison. "Um, we got there at the same time, I guess," Audrey said. "I don't remember."

Before I could try to get more information out of them, I noticed JT standing a dozen yards away talking to Meghan. Their voices were too low for me to hear what they were saying, though I could see that JT looked angry. As I watched, he reached forward, grabbed the girl by the shoulder, and shook her vigorously.

My eyes widened in alarm. "Hey!" I blurted out, hurrying toward them. "What's going on over here?"

JT glowered at me as he backed away from the girl. "Nothing," he muttered. Then he spun on his heel and stomped away.

I let him go, turning to focus on Meghan. "Are you okay?" I asked with concern, putting a hand on her arm. "What was he saying to you?"

When Meghan looked up at me, I saw that she was in tears. "Nothing," she whispered, her voice hoarse and barely audible. "It was nothing. Don't worry about it."

She pulled free of my hand and raced away, disappearing around the corner of the building. Her friends saw her go and followed.

I sighed, feeling worried and uncertain. It seemed almost certain now that something fishy was going on. My fellow volunteers and I were the only people on the island. That meant there were only two possibilities—one, that the fire had started by mistake, perhaps due to faulty wiring or some such. Or two, that someone in our group had set it.

But who? I glanced thoughtfully around the yard. Deirdre, Ashley, and Synndi were huddled together near the theater entrance. Remembering Ashley's accusation against me, I wondered if she might be trying to frame me to thwart my imaginary quest for Jake Perrault's attention.

I almost immediately shook my head. Ashley might be even more shallow, competitive, and ridiculously histrionic than her cousin, but she certainly wasn't quite that stupid. Besides, it wouldn't really explain everything else that had happened . . .

Wandering slowly across the grass toward the theater, I tried to come up with some more realistic scenarios. My mind kept returning to JT—the arsonist's relative, the silent mystery man. Perhaps Meghan had seen him set the fire, and he was threatening her to keep her quiet. But why would he want to burn down the theater? Over the past couple of days, I'd seen him put a lot of hard work into the place. Why try to destroy that? What's more, why would he have worked so hard to put out the fire if he'd just started it?

Maybe he was an incurable arsonist just like his

nephew. Was that why he'd been in jail as George had discovered? If so, that would be enough to explain the fire. But it still wouldn't really explain the money comment I'd overheard on the phone that first night. *All we have to do is figure out a good way to make the switch, and all that money will be ours. . . .* What could that mean? What switch? What money?

And speaking of money, there was also the matter of that fake dollar printout I'd found in the computer room. Did that tie into all this somehow? I wasn't sure. It seemed pretty random—the printout wasn't a good enough fake to pass for real money even if the color were corrected.

I sighed, pressing the heels of my hands to my forehead. Inhaling all that smoke just now had given me a pounding headache. Trying to puzzle through my brief list of unlikely suspects was only making it worse.

The trouble was, nobody seemed to have a motive, either for the money comment or for the fire. Deirdre and Ashley certainly didn't need money thanks to their wealthy families. Neither did Synndi, considering she had both a recent—probably very healthy— divorce settlement and a new boyfriend so amazingly clever and successful that she couldn't stop telling us about him. The three younger girls might want money, but as far as I could tell they would be the last people who would want to burn down the theater.

I barely knew anything about Wayne other than the fact that he was all moony-eyed over Synndi. In fact, he was so completely distracted by her that I had a hard time imagining him finding the time to plot against the project on the side.

Then there was JT. So far he was the only one with a suspicious past. I wished I'd been able to speak with George directly. She might have been able to give me more details about JT's connection to his notorious relative.

There was just one solution to that . . . Everyone else was still pretty distracted by the fire, so it was no trouble to sneak into my room inside the theater and grab my cell phone. The whole place reeked of smoke, but I ignored that as I quickly dialed George's number.

"Rats," I muttered as I heard the familiar start of my friend's voicemail message. I tried George's house number next, and then Bess's house, but there was no answer at either place.

Oh well. That just meant I would have to do my own research. Tossing my phone on the cot, I headed for the door. By a stroke of luck, all of the others had disappeared while I was inside, so I was able to hurry over to the B and B without being questioned.

But my luck ended there. I'd barely sat down at the computer when I heard Synndi calling my name. I leaped to my feet and grabbed the dust rag I'd abandoned there earlier just seconds before she strode into the room.

"There you are," she snapped when she saw me. "Look, there are much more important things to do right now than dusting this place. I need you to get over to the theater and help clean up from the fire. This is going to put us way behind schedule unless we all work extra hard."

I bit my lip and glanced longingly at the computer. Talk about being behind schedule—the big fund-raiser was the next night. If I didn't figure out this mystery in the next twenty-four hours or so, it might never get solved.

But I couldn't tell Synndi that. I would just have to let her keep bossing me around for a while longer. Because as far as I was concerned, everyone on the island was still a suspect until I proved otherwise.

And, of course, as any reader of my novels could point out, one of the most important parts of solving mysteries is finding all the keys to the puzzle. Until one knows all the facts, it can be next to impossible to sift true clues from false ones or make the right connections. Even one missing piece can shift the whole picture out of focus . . .

10

Fashion Victims

Back at the theater, I found almost everyone pitching in on the cleanup efforts. That was a relief. Considering my track record with Synndi, I was afraid she would order me to do it all by myself while she took the others into town for manicures.

I threw myself into the work, helping Wayne, Ashley, and Deirdre take down the charred theater curtain and drag it outside. While my body threw itself into the physical labor, my mind was busy pondering the events of the past few days.

The more time passed, the more desperate I was to figure out exactly what was going on and who was behind it. The trouble was, I had almost nothing to go on except a few weird clues and events, all seemingly disconnected. I wasn't even sure which were part of the mystery and which were just coincidences—even the fire might have been an accident. Not to mention that I had a whole house full of suspects but few plausible motives . . .

As I collected another armload of burned fabric and carried it out to the Dumpster, I found myself wishing my friends were around. Usually when I got stuck on a case, they were there to talk it over with me and help me get unstuck. But this time I was on my own.

"Heads up, Drew," Deirdre's sharp voice broke into my wistful thoughts as I hurried back into the narrow hallway just inside the back door. "Watch where you're going—I've got a whole load of stinky cheap charred velvet here, and I don't need you crashing into me and making me pick them all up again."

"Sure. Sorry." I stared at her, a sudden thought popping into my head. Deirdre. I'd known her for a long time—too long, as George would have said. She might be kind of a jerk, but I felt pretty confident in saying that Deirdre Shannon was neither a thief nor an arsonist. That made her the only other person on the island I was sure wasn't involved in whatever was going on.

I gulped, not sure I was desperate enough for someone to talk over the case with to resort to Deirdre. Then again, what choice did I have? I was certainly getting nowhere fast on my own, and time was

115

running out. Besides, while Deirdre was as shallow and selfish as they came, she wasn't nearly as stupid as she liked to let on. In fact, I had to admit that her rather devious brain had actually been helpful now and then in past cases.

I followed her out of the hallway and across the parking lot, watching as she hoisted her load of fabric into the Dumpster. She looked startled when she turned around and saw me standing there.

"What?" she demanded. "Why are you staring at me like that? Do I have ashes on my butt or something?"

"Nothing like that." I glanced around, making sure nobody else was in sight. "Listen, Deirdre. I wanted to talk to you about something."

"Is this about Ashley's stupid Jake obsession?" She rolled her eyes dramatically. "Because I don't want to hear about it, okay? If you think you have it bad, you should try being me. I mean, she only talks about him nonstop twenty-four–seven. She's totally unhinged. She kept me up until, like, one a.m. last night, debating about whether she should go by Ashley S. Perrault or Ashley Shannon-Perrault when they get married."

I shook my head, smiling. "No, that's not what I want to talk about," I assured her. "It's just . . . Have you noticed anything suspicious going on around here?"

116

"What, you mean the fire? You're starting to sound like Synndi now. I couldn't believe she was so freaked out by a stupid little fire. I mean, look at this place—there are fire hazards everywhere."

"Well, yeah, I'm partly talking about the fire," I said, biting my tongue to stop myself from reminding her how freaked out she'd been acting during the fire herself. After all, it wasn't Synndi who'd been running around screaming her head off while the curtain went up in flames. "But also other stuff," I went on. "I just have this hunch there's something weird going on around here."

"Oh, give me a break." She snorted loudly, brushing off her ashy hands on her jeans. "Don't tell me you're trying to turn this trip into one of your stupid detective games! Some imaginary mystery is the last thing we need right now. It's going to be hard enough to get everything finished before the ball tomorrow night."

"It's not an imaginary mystery," I said, feeling a little defensive. "I'm telling you, there's something fishy going on, and—"

"Look, the only mystery around here is the mystery of how Ashley ended up in the smallest room in the B and B," Deirdre interrupted. "Not that I'm complaining, of course." She smirked slightly. "Oh, and then there's the mystery of exactly what was in that slop you forced us to eat for dinner last night. And, of course, the mystery of why someone as supposedly fashionable as Synndi would decide to wear a dress for a fancy ball that hides her figure instead of showing it off—wait until you see what she's wearing! Even someone as clueless about fashion as you won't believe it."

"Okay, fine," I broke into her rant. "Maybe if you just listen to what I overheard the other night . . ."

She didn't even seem to hear me. "I mean, doesn't she know that hoop skirts are totally beyond dorky and only excusable on women with big hips?" she exclaimed, seeming completely scandalized by the very thought. "Is she trying to start some lame new trend or something? She could wear absolutely anything and look good, and yet—"

"Deirdre!" I said loudly, desperate to get her back on track. "Focus, okay? I'm trying to tell you something important. I found out there's a connection between the Riverside arsonist and someone here, and—"

"Whatever," Deirdre broke in with a shrug, clearly already losing interest in the whole conversation. "Look, there's Ashley—I promised to help her pull up the rest of that stinky old carpeting. Gotta go."

She rushed off into the building without waiting for a response. I could tell she had to be bored with our conversation if she was so eager to get back to work to avoid it. As I turned away with a sigh, I noticed JT standing at the edge of the parking lot about twenty yards away. He was staring in my direction with a quizzical expression on his face.

I gulped. Had he overheard what I'd just said to Deirdre? Even the possibility made me uneasy. It was definitely time to do a little more research on JT Jefferson. No, make that way *past* time.

This next time I sneaked away to my room to call George, I got through to her on the first try. "Finally!" I exclaimed when I heard her familiar, still slightly mush-mouthed voice answer. "Where have you been all day?"

"Bess took us out for ice cream," she replied. "That's about the only thing I can eat. I was starving to death."

"Sorry to hear that. Isn't your mouth feeling any better?"

"Not really," she grumbled. "Remind me never to have my wisdom teeth out again, okay?"

I could tell she was feeling sorry for herself. George doesn't deal with pain very well. It seemed like a good time to change the subject to the real purpose of my call.

"Ned told me you found out that JT is the Riverside arsonist's uncle and that he spent some time in prison." I dropped my voice as I said the last part, my eyes darting around the room as if expecting to find JT standing in one of the corners. I guess his sudden appearance back by the Dumpster had spooked me a little. "I was hoping you could fill me in on any other details you found out. It could be important."

"He's not an arsonist like his nephew," she said. "He went to jail for robbing a convenience store and holding up the owner, which he supposedly did due to debt from a bad gambling addiction."

"Gambling?" I repeated slowly, already trying to make that new piece of the puzzle fit with the rest. "Interesting. What else?"

"Well, all this took place more than fifteen years ago, way before the Riverside arsonist thing," George said. "The robbery, I mean. I guess they threw the book at him in a big way, though, because he just got out."

I nodded, still turning over the new information in my mind. The gambling thing added a whole new twist. "What if JT's gambling again?" I speculated. "That would explain why he needs money. He might have been talking to an accomplice on the phone that night. I wonder why he would risk calling from inside the bed-and-breakfast with all the rest of us around, though?"

"I dunno." George didn't sound that interested. "Hey, Bess just came in and started poking me in the arm. I think that means she wants to talk to you. I'm going to give you to her and go do another salt-water rinse. My mouth is killing me after all this talking."

"Okay. But if you remember anything else, be sure to—"

"Nancy?" Bess's voice interrupted. "Hi! George already took off for the sink. She's being a real wuss about this whole thing."

I grinned. It sounded as though Bess might be getting sick of her baby-sitting duty. "So how's your week going?" I asked her.

"Don't ask." She sighed loudly into the phone. "But, hey, isn't tomorrow night your glammo formal ball? Are you totally excited?"

"Thrilled," I replied flatly. "Actually, I've barely thought about that. There's too much going on around here." I quickly filled her in about that day's fire, realizing I hadn't mentioned it to George. "Did George tell you what she found out about JT Jefferson?" I finished.

"Yeah, I think so." Bess sounded distracted. "Hey, you never told me what you're planning to wear to the fund-raising gala. You were supposed to let me help you choose something, remember?"

"Oh, yeah. Sorry." I vaguely recalled her mentioning something about that before my departure. "Anyway, I just brought that floral-print dress I got last year."

"The pink-and-white tulip dress?" Bess sounded horrified. "But that's not formal at all!"

"It's okay. The info just said to dress up as much as we liked." Just then I heard the sound of voices in the hallway outside my little cell. "Look, I think the others are coming. I should go before they find me here and accuse me of slacking off. But call me if you guys think of anything useful, okay?"

The next day was our last on the project. When we arrived at the theater that morning, there seemed to be an impossible amount of work left to do before the place would be ready. But miraculously, by the time the hands on the clock over the former snack bar hit four o'clock, most of it was done. The walls all sported fresh coats of paint in cheerful colors, the new flooring had been laid in the old theater area, the donated furniture was in place, and the men had replaced the broken light fixtures and taken care of a bunch of other last-minute repairs.

"We're getting there, people," Synndi said as we all gathered in the lobby, which was now painted a vibrant shade of blue. "I think all we have to do is sweep the floors and hang the shades, and we'll be . . ."

"What about the main bathroom?" Ashley broke in. "We haven't been able to do anything in there because all of Nancy's junk is in the way."

Synndi gasped. "Oh no, I almost forgot about that! Nancy, why didn't you remind us?" She turned to stare at me accusingly.

I didn't bother to respond to that. "I'll go move my stuff," I said patiently.

"No, I'll need you to start scrubbing the walls in there so we can paint as soon as possible," Synndi announced. "Wayne can haul your things over to the B and B. Right, Wayne?" She smiled at him sweetly.

"Sure, Synndi!" Wayne said eagerly, lapping up the smile like a starving puppy. "I'll go do it right now."

As Wayne slung my bags over his shoulders and took off, the rest of us started sprucing up the bathroom. Synndi directed Deirdre and Ashley in removing the cot and other furnishings while JT got to work checking the bathroom fixtures, and the three younger girls and I wiped the dust and cobwebs off the walls. By the time Wayne returned ten minutes later, we were almost ready to start painting. Less than an hour after that, with all of us wielding paintbrushes, the ratty little place where I'd been staying looked clean and bright and almost presentable.

"Hey, too bad this place didn't look like this a week ago," I joked, feeling the first glow of true teamwork I'd felt all week. "We all would've been fighting over who got to stay here."

Deirdre rolled her eyes. "Right," she said. "Come

on, Ash. It's getting late. Let's go get showers before the brats hog all the hot water." She jerked her chin in the direction of the younger girls, who ignored her as usual.

The cousins disappeared, leaving the rest of us to touch up the last few spots and put the paint away. "I guess I'd better get going too," Synndi announced a few minutes later. "It will take me a while to get ready—it's very important for someone like me to look my best at a big event like this. You guys can finish the cleanup and other stuff, right?"

She didn't really give us a chance to answer, hurrying out of the room immediately. My heart sank as I realized we still had to sweep the entire place, put away the drop cloths and other equipment from painting earlier, and hang shades and curtains in all the windows. With the other volunteers dropping like flies, those tasks were looking bigger and bigger. Still, I knew I had to stay until it was all done. I'd made it this far, I certainly wasn't going to quit now. I didn't want to let Hazel down.

We split into teams with Audrey helping the men hang the curtains while Lacy, Meghan, and I cleaned up the painting stuff. The work went pretty fast that way, especially since all of us were so focused on getting finished that there was little talking or goofing off.

Soon after the last of the shades were up, I noticed

that JT had slipped away without a word to the rest of us. The three girls noticed too.

"Hey, how come we're still here while everyone else keeps leaving?" Audrey complained. "We have to get ready for the party too."

"Yeah, we don't want to look like we've been stuck in a dirty old theater all day," Lacy quipped.

"Go ahead if you want," I told them. "We're almost finished anyway. Wayne and I can finish up."

"Thanks, Nancy!" Meghan cried.

"See you at the party!" Audrey added, sounding excited.

I smiled as they rushed off, chattering eagerly about what they were going to wear. "Looks like it's just you and me," I told Wayne ruefully. "Come on, we can get the sweeping done quickly if we each take a section of this place. Then all we'll have to do is a little last-minute picking up, and we're done."

Wayne nodded, cracking his knuckles and then grabbing a broom. "It's getting late," he pointed out. "If we don't finish in time, are you planning to skip the ball and stay here?"

"I considered it," I admitted. "I'm not much for fancy balls. But . . ."

Catching myself just in time, I realized I'd been about to spill the real reason: I wanted to keep an eye on things tonight in case something mysterious happened. The words from that overheard phone conversation kept dancing through my head—*I already know the perfect way to sneak it out right under everyone's noses. . . . All we have to do is figure out a good way to make the switch, and all that money will be ours. . . .*

What if the plotters were talking about doing something at the gala? Maybe they were planning to steal the donor checks that would be coming in, or perhaps they knew about something expensive—a fancy piece of jewelry belonging to an attendee, a piece of art from the ballroom?—that they intended to switch for a fake. The possibilities swirled around in my head, making me dizzy and a little sick with the fact that I had no idea what, if anything, to expect . . .

Realizing that Wayne was waiting for me to finish my sentence, I forced a smile. "I don't want to miss my chance to meet Jake Perrault," I said, faking a sort of Deirdre-esque giggle. "He's totally hunky! And I'm looking forward to talking mysteries with Hazel, too."

"Hmm." Wayne looked slightly perturbed, and I wondered if I'd gone overboard with the Jake thing. "Well, I think we're just about done here. If you don't mind, I think I'll run over to the house and grab a snack before it's time to leave for this shindig."

"Oh, okay." I bit my lip, hoping I hadn't made him feel bad—or too nonhunky. "I'm sure there will be plenty of food at the fund-raiser, though."

"I can't wait that long. See you in a few."

He took off for the door, leaving me alone in the old theater. The place was very quiet, only the ticking of the clock breaking the silence. I breathed in deeply, enjoying the pleasant scents of fresh paint, cleaning products, and floor wax. Then I walked around the place, taking in what we'd done over the past few days. The transformation was pretty incredible. I hadn't really appreciated it before—I'd been too busy working on it—but we'd really turned the grimy abandoned theater into a cool, colorful place where any teenage girl would be thrilled to hang out. As I made the rounds, I took care of a few finishing touches here and there, fluffing pillows and adjusting pictures and mirrors and furniture just so.

Finally satisfied that the place was as nice as I could make it, I headed for the door. Checking my watch, I realized I only had half an hour to shower and change before it was time to leave.

After a brisk walk across the field, I let myself into the bed-and-breakfast and stepped into the sitting room. None of the others were anywhere in sight; instead, a weird, smoky odor greeted me. With visions of the previous day's fire flashing through my head, I hurried farther into the room . . . and let out a gasp.

My party dress was stuffed inside the fireplace, engulfed in flames!

11

Burned!

All I could do was stand there, staring openmouthed at the remains of the only party dress I'd brought on the trip. It had obviously been burning for several minutes when I'd arrived and was far beyond hope of rescue. The acrid smell of smoldering fabric soon brought cries and running feet from elsewhere in the house.

"Whew, what's that stink?" Ashley exclaimed, hurrying down the stairs wrapped in a bath towel, an annoyed expression on her face. "Is Nancy cooking again?"

Synndi was right behind her, dressed only in a camisole and a fitted off-white skirt that looked weirdly unfinished, as if someone had only bothered to stitch a few hems here and there to keep its double layer of fabric together. I stared at her, for a moment vaguely wondering if this was the fashion-disaster dress Deirdre had been complaining about before remembering that she'd mentioned something about a hoop skirt and realizing the odd-looking garment had to be the slip that went underneath it.

Then my mind switched back from the others' clothes to my own. What was I going to do now?

"That was my dress," I said numbly as Deirdre and the younger girls appeared on the stairs as well, all in various states of dress. A moment later Wayne wandered in from the direction of the kitchen, licking what looked like the remains of the chocolate cake I'd baked for yesterday's dessert from the fingers of both hands.

"Your dress?" Deirdre repeated. "What are you talking ab—oh!" she glanced toward the fireplace and I could almost see the lightbulb go on above her head. "Wow. Okay, it's not exactly what I would have picked out. But why'd you burn it? Seems a little extreme."

"I *didn't* burn it," I replied between gritted teeth. "I don't know how it got in there. My point is, it's the only thing I brought that's appropriate for tonight."

"Okay, if you call *that* appropriate . . ." Ashley exchanged a glance with her cousin, both of them looking amused now that they'd caught up on what was happening. Or *were* they just catching up? Could they have had something to do with burning the dress themselves? Maybe this was Ashley's way of making sure I wasn't going to give her any competition for Jake Perrault's attention tonight. . . .

Probably not, I decided almost immediately. The cousins were both pretty sneaky and selfish, but it seemed unlikely that either of them could have done this. Ashley was soaking wet and dripping bubbles all over the steps—it was obvious she'd just been in the bath. And Deirdre had seemed genuinely confused at first. I already knew she wasn't much of an actress, so that made her a much less likely suspect as well.

Then who? The dress hadn't jumped out of my suitcase and into the fireplace on its own. Someone had sabotaged me on purpose. I glanced around the room, noting who was present. Ashley and Deirdre. Synndi, who was glancing at her watch and looking impatient at the interruption. The three teen girls, who were already wandering back up the stairs. Wayne, who seemed more interested in his chocolate-y fingers than in my problems. That meant everyone was present except for JT, who was nowhere to be seen.

"Oh, well," Ashley told me cheerfully. "Guess you'll have to stay home in your usual ugly clothes, then."

I was horrified to realize that she might be right—

I couldn't go to the big fundraising ball in jeans and a T-shirt! As Bess had pointed out on the phone, even my humble floral-print dress had been verging on too casual.

"I don't suppose one of you guys has anything extra I could borrow?" I asked Deirdre and Ashley hopefully.

I should have known better. Exchanging another smug glance, they shook their heads in unison.

"Sorry, Nancy," Deirdre said, not sounding sorry at all. "I'm afraid I don't have anything at all that would suit you."

"Me, either," Ashley chimed in, smirking at me. "So sorry."

I glanced at Synndi and the teens, but I didn't even bother to ask them. Synndi was half a foot taller and several dress sizes skinnier than me, and the teens were all completely different shapes and sizes as well. There was no way anything of theirs would fit me, even if they had an extra outfit.

"Thanks anyway," I muttered dispiritedly. As the others dispersed to wherever they'd been before, I wandered over and stared at the charred remains of my dress. What was I going to do? Spotting my bags piled haphazardly in a corner of the room where Wayne had dropped them, I hurried over and grabbed my phone. I dialed George's number first, and then

Bess's, hoping for some useful advice, but there was no answer on either line. I thought about trying Ned next, but I didn't bother. He was helpful in all sorts of situations, but I suspected he wouldn't be much good in a fashion emergency.

Of course, the problem was that this went way beyond fashion. If I couldn't make it to that ball, I wouldn't be there if anything happened. And now I was more certain than ever that something would happen. Why else would someone deliberately sabotage my chance of attending the fund-raiser?

I paced back and forth across the room, trying to figure out what to do. But there didn't seem to be a good answer. My dress was beyond repair. Nobody could or would loan me anything appropriate to wear. It was too late to make it to a store in town to buy a new outfit, not to mention that the only vehicles at the bed-and-breakfast were Wayne's minivan and JT's truck, in which we were all supposed to ride to the party.

But I had to go to that fund-raiser. I was the only one who could warn Hazel that something fishy might be going on, like someone trying to steal those donation checks, for instance.

Before long the others started wandering downstairs, now fully dressed. "So you didn't find anything suitable to wear?" Synndi asked me as she stepped carefully down the staircase. She was now looking resplendent in a burgundy satin gown featuring a voluminous, old-fashioned hoop skirt that covered her weird-looking slip. "Too bad. Guess you'll have to stay home."

Ashley was right behind her, dressed in a white dress so tight I wondered how she could breathe. "Too bad, so sad," she said with a cheerily singsongy voice. "Maybe there's something good on TV tonight. Oops! I forgot—no cable."

Synndi laughed, then swept off in her skirt in the direction of the kitchen. "Hey, Wayne!" she called. "Did you load up that cash jug like I told you?"

"All done, Synndi," Wayne replied, appearing in the doorway. He had changed into a suit and tie and looked quite handsome. He gushed over Synndi's dress for a moment before leading her out to check the minivan.

I could hear laughter and footsteps overhead, and I guessed that the rest of the gang would be ready shortly. That didn't give me much time.

"Listen, tell Synndi not to leave without me, okay?" I told Ashley hurriedly.

"Huh?" Ashley had been staring at herself in the mirror over the mantel, but now she turned to stare at me. "What are you talking about?"

"I'm going to the ball," I said with determination. "I worked hard all week. I deserve to go. I may not have a nice dress to wear, but at least I can put on something other than the grungy old clothes I've been working in all day . . . Anyway, just tell them to wait. I won't be long."

I hurried out of the room without waiting for an answer, grabbing my bags on the way. Since Synndi was already dressed and ready, I headed straight upstairs to the Sunrise Suite to avoid the crush in the second-floor bathroom.

Once there, I pulled out a clean pair of khakis and a button-down shirt I'd brought in case the weather turned cool. Laying them out on the bed, I grabbed a clean towel and headed in for a quick shower. Putting on clean clothes wouldn't help much if I was still coated in ash, dirt, paint splatters, and dried sweat from the day's work.

It couldn't have been much more than ten minutes later before I was out, feeling clean and refreshed. I was towel-drying my hair at the sink when something made me wander over and glance out the window.

I was just in time to see a puff of dust and ash as Wayne's minivan pulled out of its parking spot in front of the house and took off toward the main road with JT's truck right behind it. My jaw dropped as I realized what was happening.

They were leaving without me!

Part of what has always fascinated me about such matters is trying to guess what people are capable of when times are desperate. When a true emergency or moment of truth arises, people must react one way or another, and the result isn't always what one might expect. Will the weak, retiring, shy person rise to the occasion and save the day? Will the person who has always seemed brave and strong wither in the face of crisis, praying for a miracle or a wave of the magic wand to save the day? It seems impossible to know such things until one is at the moment of decision. . . .

12

To the Rescue

I **stared out the** B and B's front door, feeling help-less. It had been about fifteen minutes since the others had left, and I was fully dressed and trying to decide what to do. Unfortunately my options weren't looking very good. I could walk to the far side of the island and across the bridge, perhaps thumb a ride from there to the hotel. But that would take an aw-fully long time. Recalling that I'd seen a few bicycles leaning against the wall by the back door of the bed-and-breakfast, I glanced in that direction, wondering how much time that would cut off the trip.

Just then I heard the sound of a motor ap-proaching. Spinning around, I squinted hopefully toward the road. Maybe the others were returning for me!

That hope faded quickly. Instead of Wayne's minivan or JT's truck, I saw an unfamiliar white sports car, speeding down the road in my direction. It turned into the B and B's driveway and pulled to a stop right in front of me.

I barely had time to wonder who it could be when the doors swung open . . . and Bess and George stepped out!

To say I was stunned would be a major understatement. I just stared as they hurried toward me. Had they read my mind somehow and known I needed help? But River Heights was an hour's drive away . . .

"Whose car is that?" I blurted as they climbed up the porch steps. Okay, so maybe it wasn't the most important question that needed answering, but it was the first one that popped out.

George glanced back at the white car. "It's Sebastian's Mustang," she said, her words a little fuzzy as if her mouth was filled with marbles. "He drove it home from college."

"Your brother? But wait—why is he home from school now? I thought he had a job up there."

"He does," Bess spoke up, answering for George. I suddenly noticed she had a slightly sheepish expression on her pretty face. "We called and asked him to come home for the weekend and babysit."

"But—but why? And why are you two here?" My

head was spinning, and I was having trouble putting two and two together.

Bess was looking more sheepish than ever. "Well, when I heard what you were planning to wear to the ball . . ." she began. Suddenly she turned and hurried back to the car. Reaching inside, she pulled out a large garment bag.

With that, my mind cleared. I recalled how alarmed Bess had sounded on the phone when she'd heard what I was planning to wear that night.

"I couldn't live with myself if I didn't try to come to the rescue," Bess said, climbing up the porch steps. "So I called George's brother to come watch the kids, and since he'd just gassed up his car, we borrowed it to drive out here and bring you this." She held up the garment bag. "Please don't be mad, but I really think this dress will be much more suitable. . . ."

She let out a startled squeak as I grabbed her in a big hug. "You have perfect timing," I told her, relieved at the thought that the evening might not be totally lost after all.

"Huh?" Now Bess was the one who sounded confused.

I quickly filled her and George in on all that had happened since the last time I'd spoken to them. They were shocked when they heard about the fire at the theater, and even more so at the fate of my dress.

"I bet it was Deirdre." George sounded grumpy. She was holding a little metal dentist's tool, which she kept using to poke at her teeth.

"Gross!" Bess shuddered as she glanced at her. "Do you have to do that?" She turned to me. "She's been digging around in her mouth with that thing during the whole drive here." She turned to her cousin. "The dentist said to lightly *massage*, George—not to pick!"

"Never mind that," I said, heading for the door. "If you want me to put that dress on instead of just going like this, we'd better get moving. The others left ages ago, and I don't want to miss anything."

We headed inside, where Bess pulled out the dress she'd brought. As soon as I saw it, I was ready to stick with my khakis after all. It was much dressier than anything I would normally wear—made of soft, almost translucent silvery fabric, it had a big, full skirt and a fitted bodice that twinkled with tiny jewels. But Bess wheedled me into it, and once it was on, I had to admit it looked nice. The dress might not be my cup of tea, but it would fit right in with the gowns Deirdre, Ashley, and Synndi were wearing.

Once I was dressed, I was more impatient than ever to get going, but Bess insisted on doing a quick but careful job on my hair and makeup. Finally she seemed satisfied.

"There," she said, stepping back and capping the pink lipstick she'd just used on me. She stared at me with satisfaction. "You look gorgeous! Quite a transformation if I do say so myself."

"Thanks. Now can we get going?" I asked briskly, gathering up my skirts for the walk out to the car.

"Wait." Bess was staring at my feet, now visible beneath my raised hem. "What about shoes?"

Glancing down, I saw that I was still wearing sneakers under the fancy dress. "Oops," I said. "My bags are up in the bedroom on the third floor. My white pumps should be in there."

"I'll get them." Bess raced upstairs, leaving me standing there watching George pick her teeth with her little metal tool.

Bess returned a few minutes later, breathless and empty-handed. "Are you sure you didn't bring them downstairs or something?" she asked. "I searched through both your bags, but there was no sign of them."

"Do you think whoever burned your dress burned the shoes, too?" George asked, with the most interest she'd shown since arriving. She poked around in the ashes with one of the fireplace tools.

"Wait," I said slowly, a vision of my room at home, swimming into my head. In it, I could see my packed suitcases, my jacket . . . and my white dress shoes, sitting neatly on my pillow. "Um, I think I might know where they are—back home on my bed where I left them."

"Oh, Nancy!" Bess threw up her hands, sounding frustrated. "I should have known. Why didn't I bring along a pair of my dressy shoes just in case? They would've been a little tight on you, but better than nothing . . ."

"Never mind," I said. "As long as I keep my skirt down, nobody will see my feet anyway. And this way I'll be more comfortable, especially if something interesting happens."

"Maybe we can stop by a shoe store on the way," Bess said. "Trib Falls has tons of them, and I'm sure at least one will still be open . . ."

Deciding to ignore her suggestion, I gathered up my skirts again and headed toward the Mustang. "Come on," I called over my shoulder. "I'll drive."

Bess and George both started to argue about that—for some reason, they don't really trust my driving skills—but they were interrupted by the roar of another motor approaching. "Who's that?" George asked. "Thought nobody lived on this island anymore."

"They don't." I stared down the road until the approaching vehicle came into clearer view. "That looks like Wayne's van. I wonder why he came back?"

Wayne pulled up and leaped out. Nobody else was inside the minivan. "Nancy!" he cried. "Uh, you look nice. Where did you get that dress? Who are these people?"

"These are my friends." I made a quick round of introductions. "They're going to drive me over to the fund-raiser."

"Oh! Are you sure? I mean, I was just there." He shrugged. "Pretty boring, really."

"That's okay. I'd still like to go." He looked kind of anxious. I wondered if his dreams of dancing the night away with Synndi had been thwarted already. I hoped at least she hadn't been too cruel in turning him down . . .

"Well, I'm just about to head back there myself," Wayne said. "Synndi just sent me back to fetch something. I can drive you if you want."

"Thanks." I bit back a grimace. So Synndi hadn't let him down easy after all. Instead, she was still just using him as her personal servant. Nice. "But I'd rather not miss any more of the party. And these guys don't mind taking me."

"Right," Bess put in cheerfully, shooting Wayne one of her most dazzling smiles. "We'll have her there in a jiffy. Thanks so much for the offer, though—that's sweet of you."

"No problem." Wayne smiled back, for a moment

seeming a little distracted by Bess's attention. She tends to have that effect on people, especially men. "Um, but listen. Can you just wait here a second? I might need your help. Thanks a million!"

He rushed off into the house before we could answer. I was feeling impatient. Time was ticking away, and I couldn't shake the feeling that something was about to happen. I just didn't know what.

"Are we really going to hang around here and wait for him?" George mumbled, jabbing at her gums with her dentist's tool. "I thought you were in a hurry."

"Quit that, George!" Bess winced and turned away from her. "What do you think, Nancy?"

"I don't know . . ."

Before I had to make a decision, Wayne reappeared in the doorway. "Hey!" he called to us. "Synndi just called me on my cell phone while I was inside. She said to tell you the new bridge is finished—just opened this afternoon, I guess. So you can go that way instead of taking the long way around."

"Really? Cool, thanks. That'll save us some time." First the miraculous appearance of my friends, and now this—it seemed my luck was turning.

"Oh, and don't bother to wait for me after all," Wayne added. "I'll be fine on my own. See you at the ball!"

He turned and hurried back into the house. With

a shrug, I climbed into the driver's seat of the Mustang, not giving my friends a chance to argue about driving. Bess had left the keys in the ignition, and I started the motor right away.

"Hop in," I called out the half-open window. "Hurry up, or it'll be midnight before we get there."

"Chill," George grumbled, opening the passenger-side door. "Look, Nancy. When Sebastian said we could use his car, he didn't know you'd be driving it. . . ."

"And he never needs to know," I said, revving the engine as Bess climbed into the back seat. "Don't worry, Grandma. I'll be careful."

Soon we were speeding toward the new bridge. Okay, when I say *speeding*, I suppose one could interpret that literally as well as figuratively. I was feeling impatient and anxious as well as a little distracted by wondering what might be happening at the fundraiser. Plus it was getting dark by then, making it a little hard to see anything beyond the beam of the headlights.

But I wasn't too worried about any of that. As soon as we crossed the new bridge, we would be in the heart of town. Then it was only a matter of minutes before we reached the Palace Hotel.

And we were almost at the bridge . . . I was busy going over potential mystery scenarios in my mind when George let out a shriek.

"Nancy, *stop*!" she screamed, for once her voice clear and loud despite her tooth issues.

Startled, I jammed on the brakes. The finely tuned sports car skidded a few yards, then jerked to a halt, quivering slightly.

I turned to stare at George. "What?" I demanded. "What's wrong?"

She was staring straight ahead, her eyes wide with shock. Bess leaned forward from the back. Her hand was shaking slightly as she pointed out through the windshield.

"Look," she said.

I looked. The car's headlights were shining out across the water of the river. Ahead, I could see the beams and supports of the new bridge stretching across the water.

Most of the way across, anyway. My eyes widened as I saw that the bridge was still incomplete—it ended a few yards short of our shore. The front tires of our car were only a foot or two from the spot where the land abruptly dropped off twenty feet above the water's fast-moving surface.

We'd almost driven right off the edge into the river!

The fund-raiser was everything I'd dreamed of. It was like a fairy tale—handsome gentlemen escorted beautiful ladies dressed in gowns of shimmering silk and satin onto the dance floor, where they twirled about in one another's arms. I was thrilled to be there, though a part of me remained worried. Would the suspicions I had come to fruition, ruining the fairy tale for everyone? Or was it all just a silly illusion concocted in my own storytelling head? Only time would tell . . .

13

A Night to Remember

I **can't believe that** guy told us the bridge was open," Bess said for about the tenth time.

"I know," George said, also not for the first time. She shifted her tooth-poking tool to her other hand. "And I really can't believe Nancy's lead foot almost ended us up in the drink. Good thing I was paying attention."

All three of us were still shaking from our close call with the unfinished bridge, even more than twenty minutes later after driving—uncharacteristically slowly—across to the old bridge and into town.

At first I'd been concerned about Wayne, planning to stop and let him know not to go that way. However, by the time we reached the bed-and-breakfast his van was gone. Since we hadn't passed him on the only road to the new bridge, I suspected that meant he must have gone the other way. And that meant he probably knew his advice was false when he'd shared it.

"Another one for the suspect list," I murmured, easing the Mustang to a stop at a red light.

"Huh?" George glanced over at me.

"Never mind." But my mind lingered on Wayne as the light went green and I pulled through the intersection, turning left on my way to the Palace. Why would he want to hurt us—or was he just trying to stop us from getting to the ball? Could he possibly be the one I'd heard on the phone? Was he plotting to steal Hazel's charity money?

The old brick clock tower in the center of town was striking eleven as I eased the Mustang to a stop at the curb in front of the Palace Hotel. Bess was back to fretting about my shoes, but I barely heard her. The hotel was glittering with lights, and several well-dressed people were disappearing through the glass front doors. I took a deep breath, hoping I wasn't too late.

"Are you sure you guys don't want to come in?" I asked my friends as I handed Bess the car keys. "I'm sure Hazel wouldn't mind even if you're not dressed up."

"No way," George said immediately. "I'd rather sit in this car all night than go to some boring dress-up party."

Bess giggled. "No need for that. We can wait at

that coffee shop across the street." She smiled at me. "I'm sure the ball will be fun, and I'd love to get a look at Jake Perrault—oh, and Synndi Aulnoy, too. But there's no way I'm showing my face at a fancy party dressed in jeans and a T-shirt."

"But we're just a phone call away if you need us," George added, holding up her cell phone.

"Thanks." I climbed out of the car, carefully gathering my skirts to avoid tripping over them. "Wish me luck!"

Moments later, I was stepping through the hotel doors into a hushed, red-carpeted lobby. The doorman pointed me down a side hall toward the ballroom, and I made my way there, being careful not to lift my skirt too high and reveal my shoes.

As I neared the gold-painted ballroom doors, which were propped open, I could hear the low roar of talk and laughter from the crowd inside. But the foyer area outside the doors was empty at the moment, and I paused to look around. The walls were swathed in rich velvety fabric, and classical music was softly playing. Garlands woven out of ivy and tiny white flowers were draped over the doorway and around the area, giving the whole place a fairy-tale sort of feel.

Very appropriate, I thought with a smile, thinking of Hazel's distinctive writing style. This place looks like it could double for a castle in one of her historical mysteries. I just hope I can help make sure this fairy tale has a happy ending. . . .

The only other decoration in the foyer was the big glass jug I'd found, which stood proudly on a fabric-draped table off to one side of the doors. A sign was propped against the jug's milky-green, translucent glass side. Its swirling hand-calligraphed letters invited attendees to donate any spare cash to the cause, though indicating that checks should be dropped off at the office at the back of the ballroom. It also said that Hazel would break open the jug at the stroke of midnight to see how much money was inside. The jug was already almost filled with bills, with a scattering of coins on the bottom.

I was carrying a tiny purse that matched my dress. It contained a cell phone, a lipstick, and a few bills. I pulled out a fiver and dropped it in the jar, tucking it as far down in the narrow neck as my fingers would allow. Then I headed for the doorway.

The ball was quite a spectacle. If I hadn't been so worried about what might happen, I would have enjoyed it thoroughly despite my usual disinterest in fancy parties. Tall golden candlesticks lined the dance floor, the flickering wicks echoing the shimmer of the overhead lights. More ivy garlands twisted up the large room's plaster columns and lined the front of the bar and refreshment tables. Fresh flowers were everywhere, their sweet scents mixing with the smell of the candles. Dozens of people were enjoying themselves on the dance floor while many others mingled along the edges or sat on gold-and-velvet chairs in the corners.

It didn't take long to locate Hazel. When I entered, she was chatting with a small group of men in tuxedos. As soon as she spotted me, however, she excused herself and hurried over, the skirt of her midnight-blue taffeta gown swishing around her legs.

"Nancy!" she cried. "You look lovely! And I'm so relieved to see you. Young Deirdre said you weren't feeling well and probably wouldn't make it tonight."

"Deirdre said that?" I forced a smile. "Well, never mind. I'm here now—I wouldn't miss it for the world! It looks like you have quite a turnout."

"Yes." Hazel glanced around the room with a smile. "I'm so grateful that people want to help. But never mind that for now—how did the project go? Synndi tells me the place looks wonderful."

"It does," I assured her. "I think the girls will really enjoy their new home away from home."

"Marvelous. And how did you find your covolunteers? Any . . . issues?"

This time I decided not to hold back. What did I have to lose? Besides, Hazel should probably know the truth in case something did happen that night. "Most of them were fine," I said. "A few were a bit . . . unusual."

I was mostly thinking about Wayne at that point. Why had he made such a point of sending us to the unfinished bridge? Now that I thought about it, it seemed awfully convenient that Synndi had just happened to call while he was inside. Maybe he'd made up the whole conversation. But why? It just didn't make sense.

Hazel sighed. "Yes, Synndi is quite a character, isn't she?"

I blinked, a little surprised. "Um, I suppose you could say that," I said carefully.

"I've known her socially for years," Hazel went on, gazing into the distance as if talking to herself. "But ever since her divorce . . . Well, let's just say that living without a rich man to support her shopping habit doesn't seem to agree with her." She caught my eye and laughed, suddenly seeming a bit ashamed of her own gossipy comments. "But I'm sure it must be difficult for her . . . In any case, it sounds as if she really came through for me this week. As did you, and young Wayne, and those lovely girls. And, of course, the whole project would have been impossible without dear Deirdre and her generous father."

"Oh?" I perked up my ears. While I was still pretty

sure that Deirdre had no connection to the current mystery, maybe Hazel was about to provide an answer to the mystery of why she'd volunteered for the project in the first place.

"Yes, Mr. Shannon's firm made a very nice donation toward the cost of the materials and whatnot," Hazel said. "But, of course, everyone involved in this project has given generously according to his or her means. For instance, I think it's absolutely wonderful that JT donated so much of his time and effort to the project. It must have been difficult for him, especially so soon after paying his debt to society. I suppose it was his way of living down that whole mess with his no-good relative—that's how I met him, you know . . ."

Hazel was talking fast, and I was having some trouble digesting all the information she was giving me about my fellow volunteers. Based on what she was saying, it sounded as if Synndi hadn't made out nearly as well in her divorce as I'd thought—financially, that is. Interesting. That made her much more of a suspect than before in the possible funds swipe, though I wasn't sure it explained the theater fire or the rest.

Then there was JT. It seemed that Hazel already knew all about his criminal past as well as his family connection to the Riverside arsonist. Did that mean something? My brain tried to sort things into a logical progression—motive, means, opportunity. Phone call, fire, theft . . .

I was about to ask a few questions about JT when Hazel suddenly turned away and waved at someone behind me. "Look, Nancy," she said. "There's my son, Jake. Come, I'd love to introduce you to him."

A moment later, I was shaking the hand of the most handsome man I'd ever seen in real life. (Sorry, Ned!) Jake Perrault was about twenty-five years old and six feet tall with lush black hair, piercing green eyes, and gleaming white teeth. Basically, he looked every inch the movie star in his spotless tuxedo. If Bess had been there, she would have swooned. Not that I know what swooning is, exactly, but I'm sure she does and would have done it.

"It's so nice to meet you, Miss Drew," Jake said. "My mother's been raving about you all week." The corners of his eyes crinkled slightly when he smiled, giving him a rakish sort of look.

"Thanks. Um, call me Nancy."

"All right—Nancy. So how did the theater turn out?"

"Excuse me, you two," Hazel broke in. "Nancy, you can fill him in. I just remembered I need to check in with the office about something."

She hurried off, leaving me chatting with her son.

Once I got over his Hollywood looks and charm, it wasn't long before I realized that Jake Perrault was surprisingly smart and interesting—quite unlike his Hollywood bad-boy image. We chatted about the project for a few minutes, and he seemed genuinely interested in hearing all about the newly renovated theater.

"My mother will be so excited to see it," he said. "When she finds the free time, that is. Her heart is big, but her time is short!"

I laughed. "Sounds like my dad," I admitted. "He's an attorney, and he's so busy he—"

"Excuse us!" A loud voice drowned out the rest of my comment. A second later, Deirdre shoved me aside so roughly that I almost tripped over the edge of my own skirt.

Her cousin was right behind her. "Hello again, Jake!" Ashley cooed, fluttering her eyelashes at him in a decidedly nonsubtle manner. "So here's where you disappeared to. And just when we were starting to get to know each other and having such a nice time!"

"Yes, so sorry about that. It's pretty crowded in here, isn't it?" Jake shot Ashley an apologetic smile.

"Well, never mind." Ashley smiled back, looking a little swoony. "We've found each other again, now."

I was already backing up, ready to leave her to her flirting. I felt bad leaving Jake in her clutches, but I figured he was a big boy—he could handle it. And I had more important things to worry about.

"Yes, but I'm afraid I'll have to leave you two charming ladies yet again, at least for a little while." Jake widened his smile to include Deirdre. "You see, I was just about to ask Nancy to do me the honor of a dance."

Already thinking about what to do next, I almost missed what he'd just said. It was only when all three of them turned to gaze at me—well, in Ashley and Deirdre's case it was more of a glare—that I tuned back in to what was going on.

"Dance?" I stammered, taken by surprise and not quite knowing what to say. "Um . . . sure, I guess."

"Great. Come on."

Before I quite knew what was happening, Jake had taken me by the arm and swept me off into the throngs on the dance floor. As we found a free spot on the floor and started dancing, I couldn't help feeling amused.

If my friends could see me now . . . I thought. I wondered what they would say when I told them about my dance with a movie star. Bess would probably beg me for every detail. George would roll her eyes and pretend not to be interested while listening to those details. And knowing Ned, he would pretend to be horribly jealous while actually using the whole thing as an excuse to tease me mercilessly. I couldn't wait to tell them.

Meanwhile, I was tempted to ask Jake whether he'd really been struck with the sudden urge for a dance . . . or if that had just been a handy excuse for a quick escape from Ashley. But I decided that wouldn't be tactful. Instead we chatted a bit more about the project before changing the subject to his mother's writing.

"I've read all of her mysteries," I told him as we swayed in time to the up-tempo song that was playing. "I haven't had a chance to read all of her latest release yet, but I really enjoyed the one before that."

"You mean *Terror in Tremayne Tower?*" He chuckled. "That's one of my favorites, too. Do you remember the scene when that servant smuggles the countess her pearl-handled pistol beneath his kilt?"

"Sure. That was a great scene."

He grinned. "That incident was inspired by a real-life moment in the life of yours truly," he confided. "When I was about six years old, I wanted this particular toy water gun and thought it terribly unfair when Mother wouldn't buy it for me. So I tried to smuggle it out of the shop by sticking it in my underwear."

I laughed. "Oh no! Did you get caught, or did you get away with it like the servant did?"

"Caught—and sentenced to many weeks of extra

chores." He shrugged. "Of course, in Mother's novel the whole thing turns out to be a red herring, since the servant is later proved to be one of the good guys. But what's a mystery without a few red herrings?"

"That's true when it comes to mystery *novels*," I admitted. "In real life, though, red herrings can be a real pain in the neck."

He raised an eyebrow. "Ah, that's right," he said. "I'd almost forgotten. Mother told me you're an accomplished amateur sleuth. Very interesting!"

"Thanks." I smiled at him, liking him more and more. He wasn't really anything like I would have expected. Based on his image, I'd anticipated a sneering, self-centered guy. But in real life, Jake Perrault seemed pretty normal, like someone I could easily imagine hanging out with my friends and me back in River Heights.

He cocked an eyebrow at me. "What?" he demanded. "You're staring at me like I'm breaking news. Did I lose all your respect with that water-gun anecdote?"

"No. Sorry." I laughed, realizing I had been staring. "I was just thinking how surprising people can be. I mean, your mother was pretty much exactly how I imagined she'd be, based on her books. But you— well, I guess I was expecting something different after seeing your films."

"Disappointed?"

"Not at all." I smiled at him. "I don't really like bad boys anyway."

"Really? Good thing you didn't know me in my younger years," he said, winking playfully. "That water gun thing isn't the only stunt I pulled as a kid that made it into Mother's novels. There was also the time I spilled grape juice on the new rug and tried to hide it by claiming the dog drank it and then threw it up. Or the incident when Mother found me with my hand quite literally caught in the cookie jar—I didn't have a chance of talking my way out of—"

I gasped. "Excuse me!" I blurted out, backing away from him. What he'd just said had fitted the last puzzle piece into place in my head. "I—I have to go talk to your mother about something. . . ."

As I turned and hurried away, I could hear Jake calling my name, sounding confused. I felt bad about ditching him so suddenly, but I knew I could apologize and explain later. At the moment all I could think about was finding Hazel as soon as possible.

"Excuse me, pardon me," I mumbled, pushing my way through the dancers as politely as I could. Finally I made my way off the floor. But there was no sign of Hazel anywhere. Recalling what she'd said about checking in with the office, I headed for the back wall of the room.

Soon I found myself in a long, narrow hallway

running behind the ballroom. It seemed to be a sort of utility area, containing the restrooms, office, and various other unmarked doorways that I assumed hid closets or passages to other parts of the hotel. To my surprise, I almost immediately ran into Ashley in the otherwise deserted hall.

"Having fun stealing other peoples' men?" she asked when she saw me.

I ignored the snippy comment. "Have you seen Hazel?" I asked her breathlessly. "I need to find her right away—it's very important."

"Um, sure," Ashley replied, glancing around the hallway. "I just saw the old woman heading through that door there."

She pointed to one of the unmarked doors. Barely pausing long enough to mumble my thanks, I raced over and yanked it open.

I was all the way through before it registered that it was pitch-dark in the room. A moment later I bumped into something that fell over with a clatter, and my nostrils were assaulted by the strong smells of bleach and cleaning solutions. I belatedly realized that I'd just rushed into some kind of supply closet.

Before I could react, I heard the door slam shut and lock behind me.

The ball was going splendidly. The turnout was most gratifying, and everyone seemed to be having a wonderful time.

Nancy had arrived rather late, but finally joined us looking quite spectacular in a lovely, princess-cut silver gown. Unfortunately, by the time I spoke with her, I'm afraid I had been partaking of some of the bartender's delicious tropical specialties, and my tongue had been loosened a bit. Due to that, I confess I made some quite unladylike and inappropriate remarks about one of her fellow volunteers. While I was certain that Miss Drew had the discretion not to repeat such gossip, further reflection indicated that I should apologize for my indiscretion as I did not want her to think less of me. Although

I'd always had my doubts about the morals of the individual in question, it simply wasn't proper to share such thoughts with others.

And so, after completing my business in the ballroom's office, I went in search of Nancy to tender that apology.

However, she was nowhere to be found. My son had seen her most recently, but could only report that she'd suddenly fled from him in the midst of a dance and for no apparent reason. That seemed odd, and I wondered if she might have been taken ill again. A check of the ladies' lounge showed no sign of her. As I emerged from the lounge, I encountered her friends Deirdre and Ashley Shannon, but they could shed no light on the mystery of Nancy's disappearance.

By then, midnight was approaching, and I decided that my apology would have to wait. It was nearly time to repair to the vestibule, where Synndi had set up a little ceremony scheduled for midnight. The cash jar had been her idea, and at first I'd been dubious. It seemed somehow excessive to ask for cash donations after our guests had been so generous in buying tickets for the ball and, in most cases, adding another check on top of that. But when I got a look at Synndi's setup, I thought that my misgivings had been unfounded. Though the glass of the receptacle Synndi had chosen was thick and cloudy with age, I could see that the jar was filled nearly to the top with bills. At that point, I was nearly overcome with the wonderful munificence of the attendees and what that money would mean to the lives of those disadvantaged girls.

By ten minutes before midnight, most of our guests were gathered around the cash jar. I began with a little speech, thanking the guests and describing the results of our project. Then I introduced Synndi and the other volunteers, and they stepped forward to take a bow. Nancy was still absent, but I did my best to push that thought aside.

"It seems a shame to break such a unique old jar," I commented as Wayne stepped forward to hand me a heavy mallet.

"It's for a good cause, Mother," Jake said as he stepped forward to assist me. He patted the narrow neck piece that was the jar's only opening. "How else can we get the money out—through a straw?"

That made everyone laugh. As the clock struck the first chime of midnight, Jake and I swung the mallet toward the old glass. The jar split with a satisfying *crack*, allowing the bills within to spill out onto the table.

The next few minutes were rather confusing. I shall endeavor to recount them as best I can. I don't recall who was the first to start murmuring suspiciously, but Ashley Shannon's exclamation was burned into my brain.

"This isn't real money!" she cried, grabbing dozens of the bills in her fists and tossing them in the air. "Not most of it, anyway. It's just life-size pictures of dollar bills printed on computer paper!"

There was a confused uproar as we all realized she was right. I heard murmurings from the crowd, some directed toward me. For my part, I was frozen in place—unlike the sassy heroines in my stories, I knew not how to react to this turn of events!

Then Synndi spoke up, her lovely features twisted with horror. "But the money has to be real! I stuck several genuine twenties in there myself when I first arrived this evening!"

"Duh," young Audrey spoke up, in the inimitably casual vernacular of today's teens. "Don't you get it? Someone probably stole the money and replaced it with fakes to hide the crime long enough to get away!"

At this, Synndi looked more anxious than ever. "What if they're after the checks, too?" she cried. "With all of us out here and nobody in the office . . ." She gasped. "I'd better run back there and make sure the checks are still safe."

As she hurried off, the crowd's murmurs grew louder. People were looking around suspiciously, clearly trying to ascertain who had left the party early. For my part, I remained immobilized with shock. Who could have done such a thing? It was like one of my stories come to terrible life!

Synndi returned moments later, looking flustered. "The checks are gone too!" she reported. "I searched the whole office—they're not there anymore!"

The situation was growing more outrageous by the moment. A few people seemed instantly ready to blame the three young teens who had helped so much with the renovation. I myself felt quite certain they weren't to blame, but before I could speak in their defense, Wayne stepped forward, looking nervous.

He cleared his throat. "I don't know if it means anything," he said. "But I noticed JT is nowhere to be seen, and—"

"JT didn't steal that money!" a new voice announced with authority. There were surprised gasps from the crowd. I turned to see Nancy Drew, standing in the doorway.

"Huh?" Wayne responded.

"I said, JT didn't steal that money," Nancy repeated coolly. "But I know who did."

14

The Stroke of Midnight

Hey!" I shouted, pounding on the closet door. "Ashley? Let me out of here!"

My only answer was silence. I pressed my ear to the door, trying to figure out if she was still out there, but couldn't hear a thing. Stepping back, I took a deep breath and glanced around. It didn't do much good. The only light in the space was the sliver coming in from under the door, which left it too dark to make out anything other than vague shapes around me.

By feeling around carefully, I found a light switch near the door. When the overhead bulb sputtered on, I saw that my initial guess was right. I was surrounded by bleach bottles, mops, brooms, spare lightbulbs, and the other paraphernalia of a janitor's closet. I searched the shelves and boxes for something that would help me pick the lock, but came up empty.

It was only then that I remembered I had one tool with me that would almost certainly do the trick—my cell phone. I pulled it out of my handbag and quickly dialed George's number. Bess answered after a couple of rings. I could hear the clatter of dishes and the murmur of conversation in the background.

"Hey, Nancy. How's the party going? Did you meet Jake Perrault yet?"

"Yes. But never mind that right now; I have a slight problem. . . ." I quickly filled her in.

There was a moment of silence. "Huh?" she said at last. "Deirdre's cousin locked you in a closet? Why?"

"Good question." I shook my head, for a moment wondering if there could be a flaw in my earlier brainstorm. "I'll have to figure it out later—after you get me out of here. See, it's really important for me to talk to Hazel before midnight. I'll tell you all about it later, but I think I've solved the mystery."

"Gotcha," Bess said immediately. "We're on our way. Tell me where the closet is exactly?"

After we hung up, I paced as best I could in the tiny room. It was close to midnight, and if I didn't get out of there soon . . .

Just when I wasn't sure I could stand it any longer, I heard activity in the hallway outside. "Bess? George?" I called.

"Yo!" George replied.

"So which door is yours?" Bess added.

I knocked on my side of the door to guide them. Soon I could hear them just outside. "Hurry, unlock it," I urged.

The doorknob jiggled and rattled. I stood there ready to race out as soon as it opened.

But it didn't.

"Hey," Bess called, sounding worried. "I don't think we can get it open from this side, either. It looks like it was locked with a key."

All I could do for a moment was stand there in disbelief, silently cursing the hotel's old-fashioned charm—and hardware. Now that I thought about it, I vaguely recalled noticing big, picturesque brass keys sticking out of some of the locks in the hallway. Ashley must have turned the key in the lock and then removed it and taken it with her.

Just then I heard the distant, muffled sound of the town's clock tower pealing out the first stroke of midnight. That brought me back to my senses.

"Listen," I called through the door. "If I can't get out, you guys have to find Hazel for me. There might still be time to stop the crime that's about to happen. You have to tell her—"

"Hey," a new voice interrupted before I could finish giving my friends the solution to the mystery.

"Who are you guys? Didn't you hear we're supposed to, like, dress up for this thing?"

I immediately recognized Meghan's distinctive teen drawl. "Hey, Meghan!" I called. "It's me, Nancy. Those are my friends—they're trying to get me out of this closet."

"Nancy?" the girl's voice sounded closer. "What are you doing in there?"

"Never mind," I said. "But my friends have to go do something for me. So could you do me a favor and find a hotel worker to let me out of here?"

The girl laughed. "Why bother?" she said.

My heart sank. It seemed I couldn't catch a break . . .

"Here, give me that thing, and I'll get her out right now."

My heart leaped again. I wasn't sure what Meghan had meant by "that thing," but the next thing I knew the doorknob was rattling again. A few seconds later, there was the soft click of gears and the door popped open. Meghan was standing there in the hall with George's little metal teeth-scraping tool in her hand.

"Voilá," Meghan said with a grin. Then she turned to hand the tool back to George. "Here you go."

"Gross." George surveyed it with disgust. "I can't put it back in my mouth now!"

I grinned back at Meghan, grateful for her lock-picking skills. Her life of petty crime had certainly come in handy this time. But at the moment, I didn't have time for more than a quick, heartfelt thanks. The clock had finished tolling out the hour, and I knew it might already be too late. But I had to try.

I sprinted down the hall and out across the deserted ballroom. When I burst out into the foyer, I was just in time to see Wayne step forward.

"Look, I don't know if it means anything," he said. "But I just noticed JT is nowhere to be seen, and—"

"JT didn't steal that money!" I blurted out. Ignoring the startled murmurs from all around me, I took another step forward. The broken glass jug was lying on the table, fake money pouring out of it. I was relieved to see that it had cracked into a couple of big pieces instead of shattering. If the latter had happened, it would have made it a lot harder to back up what I was about to say.

"Huh?" Wayne responded.

"I said, JT didn't steal that money. But I know who did." My friends and Meghan arrived behind me, out of breath and looking confused. Searching the faces in the crowd until I found the one I wanted, I pointed. "It was Synndi!"

"What?" Synndi exclaimed indignantly as the murmurs grew even louder. "You're crazy! Why would I steal the money?"

She looked so outraged that I felt a twinge of doubt. Then I glanced at the broken jug again, and the twinge dissipated.

"That's the big question, isn't it?" I said. "For a long time I didn't think you had a motive. That's why I didn't pay much attention to you as a suspect. But tonight I heard something that leads me to believe you might not have the money to support your lifestyle. That sort of situation can make people do all kinds of crazy things."

Synndi crossed her arms over her chest, glowering at me. "I have no idea what you're talking about," she said haughtily. "How dare you make this kind of ridiculous accusation with no proof."

"Nancy . . ." Hazel looked troubled, though perhaps not quite as shocked as everyone else. "You're making a very serious accusation here."

I smiled at her. "Motives aside, all the proof anyone needs is right here in this room. See, Synndi is the only person present who could have pulled off the theft. Not only did she have access to the office and those donation checks—"

"So what?" Synndi interrupted. "Anyone could have sneaked into the office and grabbed those!"

"As I was saying," I continued patiently, "in addition to that, you're the *only* one who could have stolen the cash."

I could feel the crowd's eyes upon me as I walked over to the table. When I picked up the piece of the broken jug that included the narrow bottleneck, I saw that it was still intact. Whew!

Taking a deep breath, I turned to face the onlookers. "Did Hazel just break the jug in front of you all?"

There were nods and murmurs of assent. "So what?" Wayne called out. "That doesn't prove anything!"

"Give her a chance," George mumbled, sounding annoyed.

"That means someone had to get the real money out through this opening." I tapped the bottleneck. "As you can see, it's pretty narrow. Too narrow for most of us to fit our hands through—I learned that when I first discovered this jug back at the old theater."

To demonstrate, I shoved my hand as far into the opening as it would go. It got stuck somewhere around my knuckles.

"So you've got fat hands," Synndi said dismissively. "So what?"

"Let me try," Hazel said, stepping forward.

Her hands were narrower than mine and went all the way through, but her forearm got stuck before her hand cleared the bottom of the neck. Several other people tried, including Deirdre and Ashley. Ashley's hand got stuck in about the same place as mine had. Deirdre managed to get her slender forearm most of the way down, but her elbow stuck in the opening.

"I couldn't reach too far this way," she commented, waggling her fingers experimentally. Pulling her arm out again, she shrugged and pointed to Meghan, who was watching with Lacy and Audrey nearby. "But what about her? She looks skinny enough."

I'd been expecting this. "Come on up and give it a try, Meghan," I urged.

The girl looked suspicious. "Hey, you're not trying to pin this on me, are you?" she said. "Maybe I should have left you in that closet!"

"Don't worry." I winked at her. "Nobody's accusing you of anything. It's just an experiment."

She still looked wary, but she came forward. Her small hand slipped through the opening easily as did her arm—almost all the way up to her shoulder.

"See?" Synndi crowed, sounding relieved. "Maybe now you'll drop this nonsense about me and we can find the real thief . . ."

"Hold it," I warned. Grabbing the other broken piece, I held it up to approximate the complete jug. "Meghan's arm is thin, but it's not very long. She wouldn't be able to reach anywhere near the bottom to get the bills out. If she'd done it—or one of her

172

friends, who are about the same size—there would have been real money left in the bottom half of the jug." I glanced at Hazel. "Was that the case?"

Jake answered for his mother. "Nope," he said, sounding interested and slightly amused. "No real money at all except a five-dollar bill that looks like it was up near the top. Somebody must have stuck that in after the thief cleared out the rest."

By this time I wasn't the only one casting suspicious eyes at the very tall, very slender Synndi. She was starting to look more nervous than annoyed.

"Go ahead, my dear," Hazel urged gently. "Try it on for size, and let's see if Nancy's theory has any merit."

"Yeah, go ahead! Try it!" various onlookers called out. "Give it a try, Synndi. Let us see if your arm fits."

Synndi tried to protest, but she was soon shouted down. Finally she stepped forward, looking disgruntled.

"Fine," she snapped. "Give me that stupid bottle."

"I'll hold it for you," I said, not wanting her to grab it and smash it to stop the experiment and destroy the evidence. "Go ahead."

She shoved her hand through, but stopped with her wrist barely past the top of the opening. "My arm's stuck," she reported, yanking the bottle piece away from me. "See? I can't get it in."

I frowned at her. It was obvious she was faking, but I wasn't quite sure what to do about it.

"Let me see." Jake stepped forward. Before Synndi could react, he grabbed the bottle piece and slid it farther up her arm. "No, look," he said with his most charming Hollywood smile. "It fits just fine, see?"

At that, Synndi suddenly seemed to give up. She shoved her whole arm through the opening and burst into tears.

"Fine," she sobbed. "Are you happy now?"

"I'll call the police," Jake said, pulling a cell phone out of his jacket pocket.

Synndi yanked her arm loose of the bottle and turned away, still in tears. I almost felt sorry for her. Then I glanced at Meghan, Audrey, and Lacy and remembered how she'd tried to bilk them out of the money to support their center—not to mention Hazel, all us volunteers, and the other good people in the room who'd given their hard-earned money to that night's fund-raiser.

"If you check the slip under her skirt, you'll probably find the real cash there. The missing checks too," I told Hazel. "I may not be up on the latest fashions myself, but I noticed her slip looked kind of weird. It took me a while to realize she'd left herself plenty of loose fabric under there where she could tuck her loot."

Bess nodded, catching on. "And that hoop skirt would hide it perfectly," she said. "She could walk out of here with them right in front of everyone, and nobody would be the wiser. Very clever."

Deirdre's eyes widened. "Oh!" she exclaimed with obvious relief. "So *that's* why she decided to wear that hideous outfit!"

15

Happily Ever After

So I still don't get it." Jake took a sip from the coffee cup in front of him. "What was it I said that helped you figure everything out?"

I shrugged. "A couple of things, actually," I said. "The lightbulb went off in my head when you mentioned getting your hand stuck in the cookie jar. That made me think of almost getting my hand stuck in that cash jug, and suddenly the whole thing made sense, and I knew why Synndi was so psyched about the jug when I found it—she realized it would give her the means for the perfect crime. Then I also remembered your story about hiding that toy in your underwear, and I remembered that weird-looking slip and realized how she planned to get away with the money."

There were a few giggles from Bess, George, Meghan, Lacy, and Audrey, all of whom were also crowded into the booth at the diner. I smiled too. It did feel a little weird to be sitting in a nearly empty diner in the middle of the night in a strange town talking about Jake Perrault's underwear.

The fund-raiser had broken up soon after the police had arrived, so we were keeping Jake company while his mother talked to the police and then finished up at the hotel. It was almost two a.m., but luckily the diner was open all night.

"Wait," George spoke up, her words still slightly fuzzy-sounding. "I guess Bess and I are still catching up here. But how did you know someone was planning to steal the fund-raising money at all?"

"That phone call," Bess answered before I could speak. "Remember? She told us she heard someone talking about making a switch and something about money . . ."

"Right," I said. "The trouble was, I had no idea who I'd heard on the phone. So I spent the rest of the week trying to figure it out—without much success, I must admit. We're just lucky that Synndi got greedy and decided to go for a few extra bucks with that cash jar. She claimed that was Hazel's idea, but it turns out she's the one who suggested it." I shrugged. "If not for that, I might not have figured it out at all.

Especially with all the red herrings in this case." I glanced over at Jake with a smile, recalling our earlier conversation.

"What's a red herring?" Audrey asked, looking up from her dish of ice cream.

"It's something that seems to be a clue, but isn't," I explained. "See, for a while I was assuming that everything strange that happened during the project was connected. But some stuff turned out to have other explanations. Like the theater curtain catching on fire, for instance . . ."

I glanced at Meghan, whose face was turning an interesting shade of red. "You know, don't you?" she blurted out. "You know I started that fire?"

"I had a hunch," I admitted.

"It was an accident," the girl said, tears glistening in her eyes. "I—I was sneaking back there behind the curtain to play with some matches. Really stupid, I know. The only ones who knew about it were these guys." She gestured to her two friends.

Lacy nodded. "And maybe JT," she reminded Meghan. "He almost caught you that time, remember?"

I nodded, too, as another piece of the puzzle slid neatly into place. "So that's why he looked so angry with you after the fire," I murmured, more to myself than to Meghan.

"That's not the worst thing we did, though," Audrey said abruptly, looking sheepish. "Did you figure out that Synndi paid us to go along with her when she switched the rooms?"

"No," I admitted. "I hadn't. But that explains a lot. I wondered why you guys were so quiet about that switch—you certainly didn't keep your thoughts to yourselves when it came to most things."

The trio grinned and exchanged a glance. "She wanted us to make your life more difficult, too," Lacy said. "To distract you, she said. We didn't know why, though, I swear."

"Yeah. We just thought she didn't like you," Audrey added helpfully.

Meghan nodded. "We felt bad about it later, since we ended up liking you a whole lot more than we liked Synndi and the others. We kept talking about telling you the truth, but we never did."

Remembering the times I'd spotted them whispering among themselves, I nodded again. They'd had a lot of secrets to hide.

Bess giggled. "Poor Nancy. Everyone was conspiring against you."

"Sorry," Meghan said.

"She *might* forgive you," Jake said, raising a mischievous eyebrow at Meghan. "*If* you promise not to make matches a game."

"Sure," she said, looking a bit starstruck at having a famous actor lecturing her. "I promise."

"Maybe Hazel can make sure there are some resources at the new center to help her," Bess suggested.

"Great idea!" Jake said. "I'll be sure to talk to her about it. *If* you really mean that promise," he added with another glance at Meghan.

She nodded vigorously. "That fire was a huge wake-up call."

"Yeah," Audrey added. "And she totally corrupted us into covering for her, and keeping her secret. She's a bad influence." She giggled as Meghan gave her a shove.

"Too bad Synndi couldn't see how crazy *she* was acting," I mused. "I guess the thought of possibly giving up her ritzy lifestyle after her divorce made her nuts."

"I'll say," Bess agreed. "She was so addicted to it that she was willing to rob a charity to keep it up. That's low."

We all nodded at that. Synndi had confessed to the police that she and her not-so-successful-after-all new boyfriend had concocted the whole scheme after finding out about the charity project.

"I guess she panicked when she found out about your reputation," Jake told me, cupping his hands around his coffee cup. "She was afraid you might sniff out what she was up to."

"That's why she stuck me out in the theater by myself," I guessed. "That made it less likely I'd over-hear something I shouldn't or stumble across any-thing incriminating."

"Like that fake money you found," George com-mented.

I took a sip of my water. "Uh-huh. She hoped to keep me far away from her plans with help from her unwitting accomplices Wayne, Deirdre, and Ashley. That's probably also why she worked me so hard—so I'd be too exhausted for any extracurricular sleuthing."

"And just in case, she also wanted to keep you away from the ball," Bess said, shuddering slightly. "So she ruined your dress, then tried to send us for an unscheduled swim in the river."

"Wayne helped her with both of those," Lacy an-nounced. "I heard him confessing it to the cops."

"Yeah. He was crying," Audrey added with a slight smirk.

I, too, had overheard Wayne's tearful confession. "I don't think he realized she was lying about the bridge when he told us," I said. "She'd sent him back to the bed-and-breakfast to make sure I was still there, and when he found me dressed and ready to go, he panicked and ran inside to call her and see what to do. That's when she came up with the bridge thing. Wayne was so smitten with Synndi that he didn't question anything she said. I guess she must have called him back after we left to warn him not to go that way himself."

Bess looked thoughtful. "Hmm. Okay, one more question. Who locked you in the closet?"

"Oh, that was just Ashley." I rolled my eyes. "She thought, um, Jake was paying too much attention to me. What with the dancing and all."

Jake chuckled. "Oh, dear. I'm sorry about that, Nancy. Crazed fans are just a part of my life—I sometimes forget not everybody is used to dealing with that sort of person."

"It's okay," I said. "I got out in time." I smiled and winked at Meghan.

"That was almost a lucky break for Synndi, though," George pointed out.

I shrugged. "That's how mysteries are in real life," I said. "Unlike one of Jake's mother's novels, they don't always play out in neat and tidy ways with all the clues making sense and everything. They tend to be sloppy, like this one, with plenty of close calls and coincidences and red herrings."

"Sounds kind of cool," Meghan said thoughtfully. "And it was fun helping and everything."

"Yeah. Maybe we should be detectives when we grow up." Lacy glanced at her friends to gauge their reactions to the idea.

Audrey grinned. "We'll be the greatest detectives ever. Just like Nancy!"

I smiled at them, suddenly feeling like a good influence in their lives. "If you really think you might be interested in something like that, make sure you study hard in school and . . ."

My words trailed off as I noticed someone coming through the diner's front door. It was JT, looking a bit uncomfortable in his fancy clothes. He called to a waitress for a cup of coffee, then took a seat at the counter.

"Excuse me," I told the others, sliding out of the booth. "I'll be right back."

I hurried over. He heard me coming and glanced up. "Nancy," he said, looking startled. "Didn't see you there. Was just going to grab a cuppa before the drive home."

"I won't keep you," I said. "But I might not see you again after this, and I wanted to apologize."

"Huh?" He looked surprised. "What for?"

I took a deep breath. "For suspecting you of being up to no good," I admitted softly, not wanting the diner staff to overhear. "See, I—I found out about your record and your nephew. That was enough to make me think you might be involved in some of the stuff going on. I guess I should have remembered that old rule about people being innocent until proven guilty."

JT shrugged. "No problem," he said. "I don't blame

you." For a moment he seemed ready to stop there, but then he spoke again. "In fact, that's why I'm here. Always felt guilty about how things played out—like my checkered past mighta set my nephew on the wrong path, you know? That's why I wanted to help put things right. May be too late for us Jeffersons, but not for some other troubled kids out there."

"I understand." I smiled at him, touched by his words. "I think that's very noble. Guess I misjudged you even more than I thought."

He extended his hand. "It's been good to know you, Nancy."

"Ditto." I took his hand and shook it.

When I returned to the booth, the others were still discussing the night's action. "Mother is already talking about writing up the whole adventure for *True Crime Quarterly*," Jake was saying as I sat down. "They've been bugging her to submit something else ever since her story about the Riverside arsonist."

"Hey, she should talk to Ned's dad," Bess suggested. "I bet he'd love to run her article in the *Bugle*, too."

Jake nodded. "Sounds good. I'll tell her."

"Talk about a perfect happy ending," I said with a grin. "What could be better than appearing as a character in one of Hazel Perrault's stories?"

And so there you have it, dear reader. Thanks to Nancy's intrepid sleuthing, the day was saved and the fund-raiser was a wonderful success.

Of course, not everyone involved lived happily ever after. Synndi and her beau pleaded guilty, and thanks to their attorney, Mr. Shannon, they received only light sentences, and perhaps learned an important lesson. At least I, for one, fervently hope so. I'd always known that Synndi was the type of person who never did anything without thought to what she would gain from it, which explained why I was suspicious all along of her motives for joining the project. But like the troubled girls who are now enjoying the new center, I retain hope that she can learn from her errors and turn her life around—to take lemons and make lemonade, as they say.

Which brings me back around, once again, to Nancy. Under the most oppressive of circumstances, she managed to remain on the task and help others without thought to her own gain. That is the mark of a true detective and a good person, and it's why I sincerely hope that Miss Nancy Drew always finds herself in the midst of living wonderfully, joyfully, radiantly, and oh-so-happily ever after.

star power

by Catherine Hapka

She's beautiful, she's talented, she's famous.

She's a star!

Things would be perfect if only her family was around to help her celebrate. . . .

Follow the adventures of fourteen-year-old pop star **Star Calloway**